STEVE
NETWORK

Steve Seven

Ebook format ISBN: 978-1-927060-06-3

Book format ISBN: 978-1-927060-05-6

Audio Book ISBN: 978-1-927060-10-0

www.SteveSeven.com

Publisher: Silk Road Publishing

For My Mother, Haj Khanoom.

The sun rises over an early morning in Orlando, Florida. All is quiet along the luxurious street lined with opulent homes. A sleek black BMW glides up to the largest home on the block. The driver steps out from the car; taking a few bags from the backseat, the owner walks past a line of bushes.

Steve is hiding in the same type foliage across the street from the home. He is looking through a telescope made specifically as an iPhone 6 attachment. He comes up from the bushes like submarine, scanning the area. Steve makes notes in his iPhone 6's notepad app, as he watches the wealthy man head toward the mansion entrance.

The wealthy homeowner senses something as he passes, but continues toward his front door, acting as though nothing is wrong. Out of the corner of his eye, he can see Steve standing behind the well-groomed bushes with the telescope attached to the iPhone 6 attached to Steve's face, following him slowly as he moves toward the mansion's entrance.

For a moment, Steve – wearing gold-color sports clothes and a Boston Red Sox hat – thinks he has been spotted, but breathes a small sigh of relief as the wealthy homeowner continues toward the mansion. He makes a few more notes in his iPhone 6's notepad app before stretching his long twenty-something frame.

Unfortunately, for Steve, he really sucks at spying on people. When the wealthy homeowner slash driver of the BMW reaches the mansion's entrance and opens the front door, he turns to see Steve head-on, standing in his gold-color sports clothes and Boston Red Sox hat.

The wealthy homeowner slash driver WHISTLES, sharp and loud. A large and fit German shepherd bolts from the mansion doorway, heading straight for the well-groomed bushes and Steve's not-so-well-groomed stakeout disguise.

Not waiting to see the results, the wealthy man shouts, "Get 'em, King!" pointing at the telescope attached to the iPhone 6, which is attached to Steve's face.

The dog locking in on his target, charges toward Steve – telescope still in hand, and unaware of what has just happened. Steve sees something fuzzy in his telescope. It is moving fast and furiously, zooming out to clear up the picture, he sees the German Sheppard. Steve jumps out from the bushes, turns, and runs for his life.

"Good dog," yells Steve. "Good dog, heel, roll over, play dead!"

King grabs the telescope and tears it to shreds. Luckily, Steve already removed the telescope from his face and most importantly the iPhone 6. Not paying attention to where he is going, Steve steps backward into a pile of dog poop. He begins to hop around trying to find something, anything to wipe the poop from the bottom of his shoe.

In the meantime, King is using the telescope as a chew toy. As King is distracted with the telescope – slash chew toy – Steve takes the opportunity to put some well-needed distance between himself and King. He begins to run again, falling head first into a bunch of trashcans. He tumbles to the ground.

Remembering that he is supposed to be chasing Steve, King finishes with the telescope, and resumes the chase.

Steve is now in a full-on Usain Bolt-Donovan Bailey, final stretch of long-distance-running-Olympic sprint. He is covered in trash and, again, running for his life. Despite King being a well-trained canine, the sudden sight – not so much the smell though – of leftover food is just too much for him. As King continues to chase Steve, he eats the trash falling from Steve's body.

More than enough food has fallen from Steve's body (a result of the undesired tryst with the trashcan). Overcome with hunger from chasing Steve, King stops and settles into a feast along the curb. Steve, unaware that the dog has stopped, keeps running on down the street.

Steve's kitchen is simple not very clean, and has dirty dishes piled everywhere. Standing at the sink, Steve finishes washing off the bottom of his left shoe, setting the shoe in the dish tray as if it were a plate or glass waiting to dry. Walking with a slight limp, Steve makes his way over to the couch in his small living room. The room in question is a small, tight place, with very few pieces of furniture. An Apple laptop sits on a roll-top desk. The laptop keyboard is barely visible, and a free space to sit on any of the furniture is non-existent — papers and books are strewn everywhere.

The doorbell rings before Steve can sit down.

Steve is not impressed. He looks at the door begrudgingly. Reluctantly, he straightens up his body. Limping, slightly, Steve crosses the living room to the front door. He opens the door.

Steve's frown turns upside down. He brightens at the

welcomed sight of his friend and cheerfully greets him. "Morning, Greg!"

Greg Williams shudders in pain as he walks in. His tall, healthy body is slumped over a cup of coffee.

Greg does not look his usual best. Greg looks like shit on a stick. He answers Steve, half mumbling. "Steve, please. There's a party in my head, and wasn't invited. John Williams and Jay-Z came together for a first-time-ever collaboration, at the Grammy's and they aren't holding back. That and I don't think I'm awake yet. I'm amazed I'm functional at all really, especially on a Monday."

Unsympathetic, Steve responds dryly, "Spending your house sale commission already, huh?"

"Ya, something like that. Although not as good a celebration as I would have liked. I woke up this morning French kissing my pillow. Not exactly what I was hoping for."

A chill goes through Greg's body. An unpleasant odor is picked up by his nose. Greg sniffs the air and continues, "Steve...Dude...Man what stinks in here?"

Steve shakes his head. "I'm from Boston; this feels fine to me, 'Mr. Heat Miser'. Unlike your place where I feel like I should be rotating on a spit."

Greg snorts. "So sorry, 'Mr. Snow Miser' but us Floridians don't care much for your New England weather. Anyway, the party was awesome. You really should try to-"

Steve continues talking as if Greg hadn't spoken, "And never mind about the smell. Do you want an Advil, a blood transfusion, or scissors to cut the cord on the Jay-Z slash John Williams' concert in your head?"

Greg, about to respond to Steve's sarcasm, grabs his

head in pain. "And shhh! All I need is coffee. But, man, did you miss the party of the year."

Steve sits down, puts the laptop on his lap, and tosses a bottle of Advil to Greg. Steve looks at Greg, and says, "Look, man. Don't start! You know my reasons, and I'll thank you to drop it. I've got lots of ideas going."

Greg tries to focus, wishing the Advil would hurry up and work already. "Okay, that's valid. So, are there any potential ideas...," he begins, "*bubbling* to the surface? You got something?"

Steve is already preoccupied and starts to ramble. "Ah... not quite. I was watching this rich guy over on Spooner Street to see what tips I might pick up on how he does business, but the guy has something..."

"Don't tell me you spied on another rich guy. Dude, that's called stalking, and it'll get you arrested." Greg is clearly awake and sober now, thanks to Steve's borderline criminal activity. "Dude you are not the county jail type. And let me tell you, all these rich guys have jobs – that's what they have...And that's what you don't!"

Steve waves an undisclosed hand signal in Greg's direction, "It's called classical observation, and it'll get me rich. Besides, I was just trying to learn more about him, and no, I did not get arrested again. He just...well...just set Cujo on me."

The now identifiable smell is overwhelming. Greg has to breathe - he involuntarily smells the air. "Huh, I was wondering why this place smelled crappy. Pun very much intended."

"Ha-ha, very funny," says Steve, pretending to laugh. "However, I did manage to exit the scene gracefully."

"Yeah, right. You act like I don't know you, dude. Your exits are always shitty...Ha-ha! Okay enough with the shit-jokes. If your morning of fun "not-stalking-millionaires" and 'frolicking with shit' is over with? I have an actual paying job for you. I promise, I'm not shitting you... Sorry, I couldn't help myself. Okay, enough, I'll stop."

Greg straightens up a little. Putting on his serious face, he announces to Steve his big news.

"Dwight called. He's got a wedding reception today and needs a bartender. You up for it?"

"Yeah, sure." Steve leans back on the couch, stretching.

"You sure you want to do that, he still hasn't paid you for the last two?" Greg asks quietly as he looks at Steve.

Steve sighs. "Yeah, he's an old friend of mine. I always give him the benefit of the doubt."

Greg is slightly unsettled, but continues talking to Steve. "Frankly, I think he takes advantage of your good nature, but he's your friend."

"Anyway, Dwight said he called your phone. Said you didn't answer. So much for an old friend if you're too busy to return a missed call. What, you too busy stalking to answer? Afraid you might forget to put on the call blocker, and another millionaire sets their dog on you?" Greg asks.

Steve tries to focus on the computer screen. He finally gives up, and gets to his feet. "Hey, man. It's no big deal. I always get plenty of tips at those things, and they'll carry me until he does pay me. Besides, there are usually moneymen at those things."

"Ah, crap! I can't find my phone. I think it dropped when I was running from that dog.

Across town along the street of Millionaire's row, King sits chewing on Steve's iPhone 6.

Back in Steve's apartment, Greg is awake and resigned to help his friend. "So, how 'bout it, my man. I get your attention about the gig? I know you're always looking for ideas. I'll drop you on the way to my next showing."

Steve waves a hand in the air. Without looking up, he says, "Great," and heads for the door.

Greg coughs to get Steve's attention. "Ah, Steve, you might want to slip some shoes on first, no?"

Steve looks down at his feet. He's barefoot. "Whoops! Okay, two minutes, and I'll be ready."

Steve runs for the bedroom.

Steve's apartment building is very little, very plain and located in a simple and quiet neighborhood.

Steve and Greg look to be the quintessential odd couple as they leave the modest apartment building Steve calls home and head for Greg's next meeting at the cozy and swank art gallery of Jan Bentley.

Jan Bentley's art gallery is a small cozy place, filled with small oil and watercolors, and a few sculptures. With many paintings and with sculptures ranging from the classical to the ultra-modern, in style. The gallery has some occasional visitors, but is not yet a fixture of the city's art elite collectors. However, Jan is determined to change all of this.

Jan is a petite, attractive woman in her mid-twenties. Casually dressed, she stands with her back to the door adjusting a painting as Greg walks in.

"Excuse me, Miss; I'm looking for the owner, Miss Jan Bentley." Greg says rather formally.

Jan turns around. Assuming a strong, firm business voice, she says, "I am she. How can I help you today, sir? Are you looking to add some beautiful art to add to your collection?

Greg steps forward a little. He takes out his business card, holding it up for Jan to see. Jan takes the card from Greg hand. As she looks it over, the name on the card looks familiar. She looks up from the business card and says, "Greg Williams...Hmm...Greg Williams, yes. You called about seeing some homes in the area?"

"Ah, yes, excellent. Come in to my office, we'll be more comfortable there." Jan begins to relax a bit and walks ahead of him.

They walk to the rear of the building, Greg behind Jan, admiring the "rear view."

They approach a desk where Linda Ristori, the office manager. Linda is in her early twenties. She sits with the perfect 'I-won't-ever-experience-future-back-pains-in-old-age-period' posture. She is very attractive and dressed to show off her figure in low-cut tight top, very short, tight miniskirt and high leather boots. She's got enough silver jewelry to give Dracula a heart attack. Greg almost walks into a wall at the sight of Linda and her outfit.

Casually, Jan says, "Linda, hold my calls. I have a meeting with Mr. Williams here."

Linda smiles and makes eye contact with Greg. "Sure, Jan. No problem," she says a little too nicely.

As Jan and Greg enter Jan's office, Linda takes the opportunity to check Greg out. Unfortunately, she is not impressed with what she sees.

Jan's office is efficient, yet warm, friendly; family pictures cover the desk, and photos of New York cover the walls. Jan sits behind her desk, Greg in a chair in front of her. Greg opens his briefcase.

"So," Greg begins, "This is a nice place. Been open long?"

Jan finds her business voice again and says, "The start of my second year. That's why I figured it was safe to look for a real place to call my own and get out of the rental market."

Greg tries to find his business and non-aggressive, casual sales voice, but he cannot help but sense a quick sale. "Oh, oh! I get it. You didn't want to put down roots until you were sure you weren't going to... go under, that it?"

"You got it. So, what can you show me in the... modest price range?" She says lowering her chin and raising one eyebrow.

Greg laughs aloud. He opens briefcase. "Quite a lot actually." Greg is quite chipper now. "What with the subprime "meltdown," there are plenty of homes on the market now. Would you like to take a drive with me? I have several places we can see today if you have the time. Just a quick phone call and I can arrange a few showings for you in no time. You could always look over my first before we go any further. It's completely up to you. My schedule is flexible."

Jan begins to stand up. "Well, I doubt you'd get a real feel for place from just a flat picture. I'd like to get out and see the real places. So, let's go!"

Greg likes Jan's go-getter attitude. He likes her spunk, but is a little caught off guard.

"You got it! My car is right outside. Come one. Let's go!" Greg says, scrambling, albeit professionally, to put everything back in his briefcase. Jan is already out of her chair, and part way through the doorway.

Greg follows. "Great," Jan says out in the gallery.

Both Jan and Greg have now left Jan's office. Heading toward the front door, they walk pass Linda's desk.

"Linda, I'm going to be out for a while. Call my cell phone, if anything comes up."

Linda tries to sound confident and shouts back, "You got it!"

Jan has not broken her stride. She walks through the art gallery's front doors. Greg continues to follow.

While Greg and Jan tour a few of the available properties, Steve, as promised, is doing the gig for his friend Dwight. The venue is a large and very face place with a spectacular main building, a huge deck area, and a pool. Off in the distances is a golf course. Steve stands amid the party guests of a wedding reception at a large waterside home in a gated community populated with pro golfers and their impossibly attractive wives. At the bar near the pool, Steve – dressed appropriately this time and very much blending in - is attempting to tend bar as best he can in his borrowed catering jacket and tie.

Thirty wedding guests mill about enjoying their food and drinks. Steve tries to listen in on their conversations. Occasionally, he makes notes in his flea market knockoff iPhone 6. Sometimes, he hears something, starts to make a note, and then shakes his head because he thinks it's a bad idea.

Almost too loud but still a whisper Steve says, "Nope, no way - nothing illegal! That's not for me."

The sounds of the party mix with the aroma of alcohol and the extreme wealth, which causes Steve to drift into a daydream. Soon he finds himself at the first hole of a large and fancy golf course. He is dressed in very expensive clothes, and is being driven up to the tee area by his caddy in a very large golf cart – the thing is practically a limo! Well, yes. It's a limo that has been modified into a stretch limo for the course.

Steve gets out, and steps over to the tee. The Caddy gets a ball, club and tee - all of them solid gold. Setting everything up for Steve, he even puts the club in Steve's hands, and positions him in front of the ball. Steve steps over to the ball, looks down at it, and looks out down the fairway.

"So, what do I do first?" Steve asks.

"You address the ball, take aim, and shoot." His caddy dressed in white and holding a large golf bag quietly leans back out of the conversation. For his own safety.

"Address the ball?" Steve asks clearly confused. "Ah... Okay...." Steve looks down at the ball. "Hello, ball! I'm going to hit you now. Warning – this might hurt."

Steve takes aim, swings the club - misses - and looks out into the fairway. The Caddy points at the ball - still sitting on the tee.

Steve's caddy leans in again and says, "It's still there, sir."

"Oh, yes, of course." Steve tries to be cool and says, "That was just a practice shot. Don't count that one! Now, you just watch this."

Steve takes another swing, tearing out a huge divot. Swinging again, he misses, tumbling to the ground. Laying on his back, he stares at the sky. Off in his distant reality, he hears the voices of the party guests, demanding more drinks and faster service.

His daydream ends.

"Hmm, maybe I'll stick to basketball or...something," Steve says to himself, back in reality. Fixing some more drinks, he places the beverage on tray, and begins to move about the crowd. A lanky beautiful woman reaches for a glass, but Steve catches a snippet of the conversation between two men, not far off.

Moving towards the two men, he repositions the tray in his hands, removing it before the lanky woman can take the drink. Flabbergasted at Steve's apparent rudeness, she shoots Steve a foul look that could drop wildlife. "Well, I never!" the woman says, holding her hand to her chest. Steve turns to the woman, "Well, you should some time, it's loads of fun....Look, I'm sorry. Here." Giving the perturbed woman her drink, Steve continues to move closer to the two men, determined to learn more about what they are discussing.

The first man in the group says, "Yes, I found that my return was excellent."

The second man asks, "Are you going to invest any more in the venture?"

"Well," the first man begins and then chews on his lip a little, in thought.

Steve gets impatient, shoving between the men. "Well? Are you?" Steve asks.

Startled, the first man shoves at Steve shouting, "What the-?"

The second man tries to step between them, pointing a finger at Steve, asking, "Who are you?"

The first man loses his balance and starts to stumble. He bumps into the woman Steve gave the drink. She pitches forward, hits a food cart, and it shoots toward the bride. The cart hits her right in the behind. Losing her balance, she falls into the pool. Everyone - minus Steve - rushes to help her.

Steve goes behind the bar, gets his coat, grabs his tips out of the tip jar, and slips away amid the chaos. He whips out his new iPhone and dials a number.

Greg answers the phone. "Hey, Greg. I'm done here. Can you pick me up?" Steve asks. Greg doesn't sound too impressed on the other end of the live. "Yeah, I know it's early. I...sort of...Yeah."

Back inside Steve's apartment, Steve and Greg both enter the living room. Greg says with a laugh, "So, shot down again, eh? Steve, for Pete's sake...." Steve is not amused. "I'm sorry! I was trying to learn more about these millionaires - how they make their money." Greg shakes his head. "Yeah, okay, Steve, I understand that. But, what about your rent? Did you manage to make anything?"

As Steve pulls out a wad of bills Greg takes out his checkbook and starts to write a check for Steve. "I... got some tips." Says Steve.

Greg is not impressed. "Oy!" Greg rolls his eyes and sighs. Greg looks down at the money in Steve's hand. "Look, Steve, I just made a sale today, I can help you out.

"Oh, Greg, no. You don't have to do that."

"Steve, we're buds - best buds, and this is what buds do for each other. Besides, I have faith in you; I'm sure you'll hit a good idea one of these days."

Greg gives the check to Steve with forlorn look on his face and knows he won't be paid back anytime soon.

"Thanks, man, for everything." Steve says quietly. "So, you made a sale, eh? Not many realtors can say that, these days. A good one?"

"Eh, okay. The lady seems to have money, but she also seems... cautious, which is also to be expected, these days."

"Really? You think she'd... invest in a new business?" Steve asks.

"Huh, I... don't know. But, she does own an art gallery, a really good one. I mean, the works there cost more than my car!"

"Art huh? Gee, Greg, I always wanted to learn how to paint."

"Steve, focus. It's not like she offers lessons! But, she may have some wealthy people who buy art from her. Now, if we could meet up with them, pitch a decent business plan to them, we might get some investors. What do you think?"

"I think we've got the seed of an idea! But... what can we pitch to them?"

"Hey, you're the idea man - come up with something! Just make sure that it's good, and that you've got a good presentation. Remember, it's like fine dining - the first bite is always with the eyes."

"Ah... got it. Okay, let me... think about it."

Steve works away on his laptop. Time passes quickly as he works through the morning, noon and night straight. Without stopping to shower, eat or shave, he has accumulated several days' worth of hair growth on his face. Notepad paper is everywhere around Steve. The following day, Steve heads out for another chance to observe the wealthy and learn from them. He finds his way to a smoking club - a very posh and fancy smoking club. A beautiful wooden bar serves drinks and lovely tables dot the room. Among the tables, sit ten men, all clearly men of wealth, drinking and smoking big cigars. Steve moves about the room, trying to listen in on what the men are saying, but the cigar smoke makes him sick. Finally, he rushes over to the bar, bends over it, and vomits. The bartender does not look happy. Steve is pushed towards the exit.

The double doors open to the wide and nicely tended sidewalk outside the club where Steve is thrown out on the sidewalk. He picks up his notebook, gets up, and walks off. Dazed, confused and looking like yesterday's trash Steve shuffles along to a nice little park with paths, picnic tables, and a playground area. Parents and their kids move about the area, having fun. Steve walks along lost in thought.

Steve begins to mumble. "Huh, an idea, an idea; where can I find a good idea?"

As he continues to wonder through the park, Steve begins to dream. In his mind, he see a large and gleaming room filled with many high-tech machines. A computer that looks like the HAL 9000 from the movie "2001: A Space Odyssey" dominates the center of the room.

Steve goes from one keyboard in the room to another, and types away furiously.

"Come on, computer, give me an idea here!"

"I'm sorry, Steve, but that's not possible." The computer says in an even droll voice.

"Why the hell not?" Steve asks leaning into the screen.

"Because I'm merely a machine; creative thought requires an organic computer to originate it." The computer is clearly not amused by Steve.

"Great, cool, where do I get one of those?" Steve's sarcasm is lost amid the computer screens. Hal sighs.

Hal is neither amused nor impressed by Steve. "Inside that skull of yours, Steve. It's in your brain."

"What, I have to do all the work? Then what are you good for? Good for nothing pile of junk." Frustrated, Steve steps back and kicks the computer.

"Steve, what are you doing, Steve? Don't do that."

Steve kicks it again and yells, "I'll do whatever I want, you're my computer."

"I think you should take a sedative and sit down for a while, Steve. You don't want to do something you'll regret."

Steve starts to rip the circuit boards out of the computer and tosses them aside. "I won't regret, I'll love it! I'm taking out my frustrations on you, my mechanical misfit."

"Steve, put those back. I can feel my mind going, Steve; I'm afraid, Steve, I'm afraid I'll have to take action, Steve."

Weapons pop out of several compartments around the room and point at Steve. "What the-?"

"Okay, buster, you put those back, or you're history!" Commands the computer.

Steve starts to furiously put the circuit boards back into the computers, changing his tone of voice. "Yes, sir, yes, sir!"

Steve wakes up from his daydream at the edge of a duck pond just before walking into the water.

"Huh, maybe I should try and come up with an idea on my own!" He says to himself. Several kids run around near Steve. He stops and looks off at a nearby tree. There's a spider's web there, and he stares at it. He sees the kids chatting happily away as they clearly decide what game to play. Steve smiles, jumps in the air, spins around and bolts back the way he came. "Yes, an idea," he shouts. "A good idea - a truly great idea!"

Back at Steve's apartment, Greg sits on the couch. Steve sits at his desk and works on his laptop, which is hooked up, by cables, to the TV. A bit of animation finishes playing on the screen. Steve turns off the TV, turns to Greg and says, "So, what do you think? You think it's a winner?

Greg slowly nods and begins to smile for the first time all day. "Not bad, Steve; I do think you've got a real winner there. You do all that in a week?"

"Yeah. A couple late nights was all it took. So, what's our next move on this?"

"Well...," Greg begins, "how about I line up a meeting with some people as potential investors? I'll talk to that gallery owner...ah, Jan Buckley or Buckman, or whatever her name is. Maybe she'll let us use her place."

Steve seems to agree. "Yeah, that's what I'm talking about - money men, and women!"

Greg is pleased. "You got it. In fact, I think I know a couple people local who might bite at this. Oh, and by the way, Dwight called to say that he's not going to be hiring you anymore. He got too many complaints from that... wedding incident."

"Ah, I thought that might happen. Well, maybe I won't need his jobs any more. You think?" Steve asks with a hopeful look on his face.

"Steve, it is a definite possibility. This is a good idea you've come up with."

Steve acts relieved and a little confident for the first time in a long while. "Yeah, if this deal works out like we figure, we won't need his 'crumbs' any more, will we?"

"No, you got that right, Steve. I'll make some calls and see about setting up a presentation. Oh, I also have some big news!"

"Well, let's hear it. You're grinning like the Cheshire cat, so I can only assume it has something to do with sex."

Greg looks devilish as he explains, "That is does, my friend. Last week I went to the local theater to see a show. Well, you remember Jessica Hart. She had a part in "Sound of Music" a couple years back."

Steve tries to remember. "Jessica, Jessica... Oh yeah, she played the oldest of the Von Trapp kids. Cute kid, she just about stole the show."

"Yeah, well now she's really something - else. She's all grown out, I mean up. Actually, I mean both! She's twenty and she was in the show. We got together after the show, and we've been dating ever since."

"Jessie's twenty! Oh, God does that make me feel old. Whoa, and you two are dating?"

Greg puffs out his chest. "Why not? We're both over the age of consent and I hope she consents soon. You should see the legs and ass on her. All those years of dance class paid off."

Steve is still skeptical. "Really? Well, good luck with her, man."

"Thank you, thank you - here's hoping. Anyway, I'll be in touch once I've got us a venue." Greg gets up and exits. Steve picks up his laptop and starts to type away. He stops, looks off into the distance, and starts to daydream.

"Huh, a success. Now... what could we do with some major money?"

Nearby sits a huge and richly decorated home sitting on the shores of a lake. Inside, we see a long room with an equally long table and many chairs. Steve sits at the head of the table; it's full of all kinds of food. A butler, quite the prim and proper English butler waits on him.

"Here you are, sir, caviar." Announces the butler and serves Steve, who eats the caviar with a grin - and gags.

"Eww, yuck, blah! What is that stuff anyway?"

"Fish eggs, sir. Would you care for the calamari?"

Steve shrugs and gives into the offer. "Ah... okay, I'll try that."

The butler stands back with an extra napkin draped over his hand as Steve tries to eat the calamari.

"So, what's this stuff?" Asks Steve pointing to another dish.

"Squid, sir." The butler is bored now and rolling his eyes at each question. Steve tries the squid. Steve spits the squid out.

"Blah! Yuck, what's with all this fishy food?" Steve picks up some escargot and tastes it. "What about this, what's this? Hmm...kind of... rubbery."

"Escargot, sir." The butler says.

"Sounds fancy. What's that mean - in English?" Steve asks

inspecting the food.

"Ah... snails, sir." Says the butler leaning back holding out yet another napkin. Steve spits out the snails.

"I don't eat stuff I would use for bait! God, don't you have some non-fish stuff?"

The butler serves him pate de foie gras.

"Try some of this, sir; it's quite good."

Steve eats some, but clearly doesn't like it.

"Takes like some kind of raw meat! What... is it?

"Pate de foie gras." Announces the butler.

"Another fancy name; sounds expensive. That Latin for something?" Asks, Steve.

"It's French, sir. It means goose liver."

Steve spits out the foie de gras. "Goose - liver? I don't eat liver period!" Steve sits up in his chair in his apartment and shakes his head.

"I need a pizza..."

Steve holds his iPhone and plays a game on it. The doorbell rings. He puts down the iPhone, heads to the doors, and opens it.

Greg and Jan enter.

"Wha...? Well hi there. Who might you be, dear lady? Greg, this isn't Jessica, is it?" Steve asks.

"Who?" Jan interrupts.

"Nothing, Jan. No Steve, this Jan Bentley, the gallery owner. She lives nearby, so I thought we could carpool to her place. For one thing, I figured you could answer any questions she has about the proposal," Greg finishes.

Steve nods in agreement, "Oh okay. I got ya," Steve responds. He offers his hand to Jan. "Pleasure to me you." Jan and Steve shake each other's hands.

"Pleasure to meet you, too, Steve. Greg gave me a few details on your company proposal; I think it's a winner."

Steve moves to his desk and picks up his laptop.

"Thanks, Jan. I appreciate that. Okay, so, folks. Let's get down to business. Greg said that you're willing to let us do our presentation at your gallery. That about the size of it, Jan?" Steve asks.

"Yes, I've got things all set up, and about twenty investors ready and waiting to hear your pitch," Jan replies.

"Okay, then. Let's roll!" Steve says jumping up. He gathers his things and exits the apartment. Greg and Jan follow him out, smiling at Steve's excitement and enthusiasm.

Several rows of seats are set up facing a large TV screen. Twenty people sit in the seats, and Steve has his laptop connected to the TV. Among the group is Hillary James, a beautiful woman in her mid-40. Greg stands next to the TV and uses a laser pointer on the screen. Jan stands off to the side and watches. In the center row, the millionaire we saw un-leash his dog now sits silently waiting for the presentation. He sits wearing sunglasses and playing with Steve's chewed up iPhone6.

The screen goes black, the "B & L Logo" comes up, and Greg gives a little bow. The people all rise and applaud, and then move to give their congratulations.

Everyone starts to mill about, and Linda moves forward to offer refreshments. She eventually slides up next to Jan and hands her a drink. Hillary talks to Steve at length; he clearly has a lot to say. In the background, we see the millionaire leave Steve's iPhone on his seat and walks away smiling. Greg sees the phone, snatches it and slips it to Steve as he walks by him.

"Well-well," Linda begins, "Jan, looks like Mr. Geekoid is going to be the next Bill Gates. You going to grab onto him before someone else does?"

"Linda, behave! Goodness, there are things in this life more important than mere money." Jan is slightly nervous now.

"Spoken like someone who never had to worry about money." Linda sneers.

"Look, he's got a good proposal, but that doesn't mean he's going to make a million." Jan is looking at the floor now, thinking. "Hey, if he makes any money, he should be happy."

Linda leans in and half whispers. "How very supportive of you, Jan."

"Hey, just being honest. Now, come on, let us do our part to win over some investors. Just because I'm realistic doesn't mean I'm not hopeful."

Jan and Linda chat with the investors. Hillary continues to speak to Steve as Greg joins them. Jan watches Steve and Hillary suspiciously.

Hillary is being slightly flirtatious with Steve and says, "Well, gentlemen, I am impressed. Who was your design team?"

"Team?" Steve asks.

Greg says pointing at Steve and himself.

"You're looking at...them."

Hillary can't believe it. She is pleasantly surprised. "You? You two guys."

"Well..." Steve replies, stammering. "It was a joint effort. Greg comes up with ideas, and I... sort of... massage them."

"Ah...That's putting it politely!" Greg says jumping in, and smiling. "I'm the 'people person'. I'm good at 'pressing the flesh' - as they say. Steve is the real idea man, and then he turns those ideas into reality."

Hillary lifts her chin for a moment of thought. "Huh, a partnership with no senior partner, and no egos clashing. Boys...I must say. I am very much impressed.

Hillary takes out two of her business cards and hands them to Greg and Steve. Jan begins to ignore the guests and watch Steve and Hillary with more intensity.

Greg down at the business card slightly confused. "What's this all about? We already have your info."

"Because, I want to do more than invest in your company. Boys, I think you have real potential. Call my office, talk to my assistant, and let's set up a meeting."

"Ah..." Says Steve just realizing what happened.

"You got it!" Greg says, nodding.

Hillary moves off. Greg and Steve look at each other, give each other a high five, and watch Hillary go - she is quite the fine-looking woman.

Jan steps up to Steve and hands him a drink and an appetizer. He takes both, eats the appetizer in one bite and wipes his mouth with the back of his hand.

"So, when do we eat?" Asks Steve.

"Ah, Steve, this is it - finger food is all they serve at these sorts of things." Gregg leans over and pats Steve's belly.

"Finger food? That was barely a pinky! Sheesh, okay, if that's how it's done. Guess I'll slip over to McDonald's and grab a burger."

"Hey, tell you what, Steve. How about lunch - on me - to celebrate the kick off to your new business enterprise?" Jan says leaning into Steve flirtatiously.

"Ah... sure. Okay, what's your preference - Mickey-D's or Burger King?"

Jan rolls her eyes and takes him by the arm.

"Ah... leave it to me. I'll find us something nice."

Sometime later and with much fanfare, Jan ushers Steve into an appropriate restaurant - a small, simple cafe on the shore of Lake Eola in downtown Orlando. Steve and Jan sit at a table, looking over menus.

"Well, so, what do you think, Steve? This okay with you?

"Sure, nice place and they serve burgers."

"Glad you like it. And, what about the company, you think it's going to be a hit?"

"Maybe. We'll have to see. My attitude is, hope for the best, but plan for the worst," Steve says.

"Very reasonable of you. I've known a lot of people who are convinced that their scheme will net them millions, and all they have to do is sit back and wait for it to roll in. That's not how my dad made his money, and it's not what he taught me!" Jan replies.

"Good for him. I hope I'm able to do the same for myself one day," Steve says.

"We can only hope. For now, let's live in the moment!" Jan responds.

Jan looks at Steve intently. Steve becomes serious and quiet.

Steve and Jan order, get food, eat and talk.

"I'm curious, Steve. How'd a Boston boy like you end up here?"

"I'm not a complete stranger. My mother was born and raised here."

"Southern Belle and Yankee Boy linking up? Oh, that must have been a fiery mix," Jan says laughing

"Oh yeah. Dad told me it was six years before she stopped saying "damned" whenever she'd say Yankee. When my Dad retired, my Mom convinced him to move here. Said she couldn't take another New England winter. I was still in school, but my siblings were grown, so it wasn't a big deal to move us down here."

"Wait, your Dad retired, but you were still in school?"

"I was a late baby; he was fifty when I was born."

"Oh, man! I can see it now; I bet he was strutting around like a peacock when you arrived."

Unsettled and nervous, Steve continues.

"Yeah, quite the affirmation of his virility. The family always said, he'd take me for walks in my stroller, and people would ask if I was his grandchild. He was so proud to announce that I was his! Anyway, we moved to Sarasota, Dad insisted on being near the water. That's where I graduated from high school."

"Is it nice down there?"

"It's okay, but back then it was quite the retirement community. That made growing up there a rather interesting lifestyle," Steve says.

"In what way?" Jan asks quietly.

"Well, when I went to college my friends said I talked like an old person. I guess it was like those stories you hear about kids raised in the wild by wolves. I didn't play basketball, I played shuffleboard. How many sixteen year-old boys do that?"

Laughing Jan says, "That is priceless; you should write a book about that. It would be hilarious."

"Yeah, that would be funny. But me, a book…I don't…" Steve says before pausing and then,

"Huh, you know something… that might not be such a bad idea."

Steve rubs his chin as he gazes off and gets lost in thought. Silence.

"Ah… so, how'd you end up here in Orlando?" Jan asks, trying to recover the conversation.

"Huh, what? Oh, my Mom and her parents died in a car accident. They left us their house, and Dad decided Sarasota was too boring for him," Steve answers.

"I'm sorry to hear that.

So… is he… gone now?" Jan asks quietly.

"Yeah. No regrets. He lived a good long life, and we had our share of good times," Steve says chuckling, looking off into the distance and away from Jan to hold back his true emotions.

Over the next few days, Steve and Jan are inseparable.

They spend time at her gallery looking at art, have dinner in small cafes, and walk through parks together. After a week, they find themselves entering Kelly Park for an afternoon together. Kelly Park is a nice little state park nestled among many large trees. A winding road leads up to the main entrance where a little shack with two park rangers inside, guards the entry to the park.

Steve and Jan drive up in her nice car. A Ranger steps up to her window. They talk, and she hands him two dollars. She drives in.

Many parking spaces are spread throughout the area, separated by trees, picnic tables and play areas. A concession stand is off to the right, and sidewalks wind and run throughout the area.

Jan pulls into a free space, and parks the car. She and Steve get out of the car, grab towels, a cooler and picnic basket, and head over to a nearby picnic table.

"Wow, this is such a cute place, Steve! I never knew about it," Jan says ecstatically.

"Oh, that's pretty normal. Most people don't. When you live in the shadow of the mouse, anything less than a theme park usually doesn't rate too highly. This is the place, my grandparents used to take me when I was young," Steve answers.

"Okay, so, what do we do first?" Jan asks, rubbing her hands together.

"Let's get wet! A couple swims in the spring, and then I'll cook us up some lunch," Steve answers, with equal enthusiasm.

"A spring? They have a spring here? I mean, it's a real

natural spring?" Jan says excitedly.

"Come on, I'll give you the grand tour." Steve chimes in and announces.

Steve and Jan slip off their clothes to reveal bathing suits. Steve takes Jan's hand and they walk off toward the concession stand. Later, they make their way to Rock Springs. Rock Springs is a long and rambling bayou of swiftly running water. It starts up at a roped off cave, flows through trees and shrubs, under a footbridge, pass an artificial beach, and on through more trees down to another footbridge.

Steve leads Jan along a wooden boardwalk up to the cave. Many people of all ages run and play in the water and on the boardwalk, all in bathing suits.

Steve and Jan reach the cave. The water looks cool and clear—very inviting.

"Wow, that water is like... so clear! How is that possible?" Jan asks.

Steve points at the cave. "That. The cave. The water comes up from a deep underground aquifer; it's almost perfectly pure."

Steve moves to the edge, and jumps right in. Other people around him do the same - some do it rather slowly and cautiously. Steve bobs to the surface.

"Wow, it looks great! So, how is it?" Jan asks.

"Great!" Steve replies.

Jan smiles, moves to the edge and jumps in. She practically shoots straight up out of the water, her arms clamped tightly around her. She shudders.

"Ohhhhh God! Oh my God, oh my God! Oh - God!"

Steve Network

"Something wrong, Jan?" Steve asks.

"It's freezing! Good God, why on Earth didn't you tell me?" Jan says.

"Jan, calm down It's not freezing, it's fine," Steve responds.

Jan splashes him. "Maybe to you. Mr. New England Boy! But to me, it's friggin' cold!"

"Aren't you from New York?" Steve asks, slightly confused by Jan's behavior.

"Yeah - well - I... have... thin blood! So... there." Jan says turning way.

Steve rolls his eyes, moves closer to Jan and wraps his arms around her. He begins to rub his hands up and down her arms.

"There, that better?" He asks.

Jan turns up her nose; pulling away from him, she turns around.

"It's... all right."

Jan spins around. Pushing Steve, she dunks his head under the water. She doesn't wait for Steve to resurface, swimming off down the creek. Steve pops back up to the water's surface, and swims after her.

"Oh, now you're going to get it! You're dead, young lady!" Steve yells, playfully after her.

Jan squeals and swims faster on down the river. Steve follows, and they eventually get alongside the beach area. A little girl stands off to one side, crying. Steve stops chasing after Jan. He turns his swim towards the little girl; increasing his speed, he draws closer and closer to her, finally reaching her. He gets out of the water onto the faux beach, running towards the little girl's side.

"Hey, little lady. What's the matter? You okay?" Steve asks softly and reassuringly.

Scared, the girls tells Steve, "I lost my mommy and daddy!

Jan stops and looks back. She sees Steve approaching the little girl on the faux beach. Swimming up to the beach, she gets out of the water, and walks toward Steve and the little girl. Reaching the two, Jan stands next to Steve, and asks, quietly, "Steve, what are you doing?"

"Just helping this little girl in trouble," Steve answers.

"Steve, you really shouldn't. These days, you try helping a kid, and next thing you know, you're getting charged with trying to abduct them! Leave her alone."

"I understand that. But we have to do something!" He says with passion and conviction. "How about this, you stay with her, and I'll go find a park ranger?"

"Okay, that'll work," Jan says, nodding her head in agreement.

Jan moves to stand next to the little girl. Steve avoids the water, and decides to run up the beach. He gets to the sidewalk parallel to the river, and starts walking, brusquely, towards a concession stand. A young couple are walking toward Steve. Steve can tell they look very worried and concerned about something.

Steve approaches the couple, carefully asking, "Excuse me? Are you looking for someone?"

This question surprises the mother, "Ah... yes, yes! Yes, we are! How did you...?!"

Steve stands still for a moment, looking at the parents

intently. "I just thought. You know...You have that look...
That look of worry."

"Our daughter, she's wandered off!" The father replies,
quickly and without hesitation.

Steve gestures for them to follow him and walks off.
"Come on, I think I found her."

The father is walking quickly next to Steve. "You...found
her?"

Steve leads them back to the beach.

"Well, my girlfriend and I did, and I was going to alert the
rangers, when I saw you. I sort of had the feeling that you
two might be her parents."

They see the little girl, and she sees them. They run to
each other and embrace.

"Oh, sweetie! We were so worried about you. Don't
ever do that again, okay?!" the Mother says in a kneeling
position, holding the child close as she strokes her back.

"What did we say about wandering off, young lady?! You
almost gave me a hernia. Don't ever wander off again like
that again!" the Father says with tears in his eyes. He picks
up the little girl, resting her head on his shoulder, kissing her
forehead, and then the top of her head.

"I'm sorry, but I'm okay now. They helped me find you,"
the little girl replies.

The MOTHER looks at Steve, taking his hand in both of
her, "Thank you. Thank you so much."

"Glad to have helped." Steve tries to hold back his
emotions. He feels like he is about to cry.

Luckily, Jan steps up to his side. He turns, looks her in

the face and says, "Come on, Jan. Shall we go? I think everything's okay now."

"Yeah. You folks have a nice day, now. And you take care little one. Try not to give your parents anymore heart attacks for the rest of your life, cool?"

"Cool," the little girl says. Jan reaches out for a low five. The little girl smacks Jan's hand.

Steve and Jan walk away, and move off toward the creek. The young family waving at their backs.

"I'm glad that turned out okay," Steve says relieved.

"Yeah, sometimes it doesn't though. Still, you took a chance there Steve. They could have thought you tried to snatch their kid," Jan replies, unimpressed, but happy to have reunited the family.

"I know, but sometimes you have to do what's right! That's something my taught me. Now, come on, slow poke. Let's turn that frown upside down, and have some fun, no?!"

Jan wraps an arm around Steve's neck. Placing a kiss on his forehead, she ruffles his half-wet hair.

They enter the creek.

Jan and Steve swim off.

Steve and Jan swim together going down the rambling bayou several times. After finally getting tired, and ready to eat, they return to their picnic table. Steve dries himself off, before preparing to make lunch.

After grilling some burger and hot dogs, while Jan sit on the picnic table nearby watching him, the couple eats. They chat, getting to know each other some more, waiting for their food to digest. Then, they head back to the water to swim some more.

With the sun dropping in the sky, Steve and Jan load up the car and prepare to leave.

"Well, that was loads of fun, Steve! We should do something like this again," Jan says.

They get in the car. Jan drives off. Steve whips out his iPhone and flips through some notes.

"Sure, stick with me, Jan. I got this town wired! I know every... ah...well, *economical* way to have fun that there is," Stave says quietly.

Jan cannot help but laugh. Jan briefly turns to Steve, and then puts her eyes back on the road. "Hey, nothing wrong with watching your money, Steve. That's something *my Dad* taught me! What you doing there?

"Just writing up some notes on some...ideas I have. I'm always looking for new...ideas."

"I see. Well, I've got some ideas of my own! What you doing next weekend? There's a farmers' market coming up. Want to go?"

"Market? Ah... what sorts of things do they do there?"

"Oh... you'll see."

The following weekend, Jan takes Steve to the flea market. It has a large open area. The roof is the only solid part to the structure, inside are small partial, temporary walls, creating individual stalls that separate each of the vendors.

Many people mill about. Jan walks along, checking out the fresh fruits and vegetables. Steve follows, weighed down with bags. He looks off, lost in thought, but doesn't seem bored.

"Steve, you okay?" Jan asks.

"Huh, what?" Steve answers.

"You seem kind of... distant. Are you bored?" Jan asks.

"No, not at all. Just... thinking about...stuff," Steve says.

"Really? I mean, you're okay with...shopping?" Jan questions.

Steve begins to laugh. Steve turns to Jan and says, "Yes, Jan. I'm fine with it. If it makes you happy, I'm happy. Besides, it gives me time to think. I just sort of... organize my thoughts and...stuff."

"Wow. I've got to say, Steve, you've never been like most guys I've dated. Some of them, God, they would rather die than go shopping."

Jan and Steve continue through the flea market grounds. They come to a booth that is a business venture. Jan moves on, but Steve stops. He sets down the bags, and whips out his iPhone. He types in some notes and picks up a brochure about the business.

Jan and Steve's time together drifts into the evening as they walk hand in hand through a restaurant with an opulent dining room. A lovely dinner table and chairs sit in the middle of the room. Classic furniture and fixtures line the room's perimeter.

After placing their orders, and receiving their meals. Jan and Steve have dinner by candlelight.

"I'm not saying we knew where my uncle was headed when he died." Steve says. "But, we did bury him in an asbestos suit with a fire extinguisher in each hand."

Laughing, Jan says, "You're priceless, Steve. I love a man

who can make me laugh."

"Well, humor's always been my... release. My way of... dealing with stress."

"Oh, so you're stressed right now, eh? I make you... stressed?"

"You make me feel a lot of ways; stressed is the least of them! I propose a toast to you, Jan. This sure is one outstanding dinner."

"Thanks," she says, pausing. "I'm pretty good at making breakfast too."

"Really? Well, I'll have to come over some time and...Oh! Okay, then."

Steve jumps up, grabs the bags, and heads for the door. Jan follows after him; smiling at his excitement and enthusiasm.

Jan's bedroom is small, brightly decorated, but not too fancy. A nice bed sits against one wall, and beautiful picture windows look out over her patio and pool area. But the view is irrelevant to Jan and Steve as they make love. In the morning, Jan nuzzles his ear – it's almost noon and they are still in bed.

"Steve, why do you have red paint behind your ear?" Jan asks, puzzled.

Steve, shocked by the discovery, replies.

"What? Oh, that, just doing a little work around my apartment. Must have missed it when I was cleaning up the other day. You know how it is, when you're a bachelor - you don't exactly...bathe regularly."

"Yeah, I know that only too well. Okay, why don't you hop

in the shower and I'll start breakfast?"

Steve goes in the bathroom. Jan gets up, puts on a robe and heads for the door. A cell phone rings. She looks around and finds the phone in the back pocket of Steve's pants.

"Hello, Steve's pants, he's not wearing them right now, can I take a message for him?" Jan says.

"Oh, hi, Greg. What's up?

He's taking a shower, I'll tell him to call you when he gets out.

No, I'm not giving you details, you pervert."

Jan laughs and hangs up.

Inside Jan's art gallery, Jan and Linda stand by a table near Linda's desk. It has a coffee pot, creamer and sugar on it. Each of them has a cup of coffee.

"So, you went ahead and nailed the geek, huh? How was it, you going to see him again?" Linda asks, raising her eyebrows, Dwayne Johnson-style.

"Linda, it was just a bit of fun! Yeah, okay, we met, I like him, and we made it - that doesn't mean it's... true love. I mean, maybe something will... grow out of this, but... who knows, you know?"

Anne Bentley, a regal woman in her 50's, enters in the background. Jan and Linda don't see her. Anne is fighting the aging process tooth and nail. She is dressed in a fabulous outfit. She has an air of superiority about her.

"Discussing another doomed relationship, Janice?" Anne says.

Jan spins to face Anne.

"Mother, what in the world are you doing here?" Jan asks,

horrified.

"Didn't you get my message? I called and said I was arriving today," Anne replies, unimpressed.

"Ah, that's my fault. I meant to tell you she called again. This time to say she was flying in to town for a visit," Linda chimes in.

"I wish you'd remembered, Linda. I'd have arranged to... oh, I don't know - be out of town!" Jan replies unimpressed, and still horrified.

Anne's expression turns cold and she says, "Well, it's nice to see you too, my dear."

Linda senses the tension. "Sorry, Jan, I screwed up." Lind shrugs her shoulders.

"It's okay," Jan begins. "I just would have liked time to prepare for her arrival; like getting some cloves of garlic to wrap around my neck!"

Linda sees an opportunity to make her exit from the now extremely awkward situation. "Okay then, I'll just leave you two alone. Nice to see you again, Mrs. Bentley."

Linda walks away. Anne ignores her. Anne turns to Jan. "You could have at least acknowledged her existence, Mother. She was trying to be nice," Jan says perturbed in a loud whisper.

"Janice, really. Come now, she's only your secretary," Anne says annoyed at being corrected; a distinct smirk on her face and slight arrogance in her tone of voice.

"She IS NOT my secretary! She is my assistant AND my friend. AND, as far as I'M concerned, there is nothing "ONLY" about her!" Jan responds, standing her ground.

Anne is not in the mood to argue with her daughter, especially when knows she's right. "Whatever you say, my dear. Whatever you say."

"You got that right! Now that we've dispensed with the opening salvo. Can I offer you some coffee? It's not espresso, but it is a nice French roast," Jan says.

"No thank you, dear.... So...this is...," Anne starts, clearing her throat trying to find the right words. "...Your gallery? You have quite some...how shall I say? "Interesting" pieces for sale here, dear."

"Thank you. I know they'll never measure up to your standards, but I like them. Now, what do you want? You didn't fly all the way from the Hamptons to discuss art."

"No, I didn't. I'm here on some business." Anne looks at a painting.

"I'm meeting with some studio executives about a merger and thought I'd take the opportunity to drop by. You never reply to my calls or e-mails anymore."

Jan is not amused. "There's a reason for that, Mother. We have nothing more to say to each other! I told you that I'm going to live my life my way, without any interference from the family!"

"Interference?! Janice, what has happened to you, what turned you against us?"

"Oh, Mother, please. Take your pick, the stupid coming of age party, you threw me, those insipid jerks with silver spoons up their butts you forced me to hang out with only because of their parents. Mother, Mom, I love you and John and Kelly, but-"

Anne interrupts her daughter quickly, "But you would

rather live here, in Orlando, Florida. A place so empty they think a giant rat and a killer whale are the height of culture and society."

"Oh, Mother, there's more than mere…-"

"And you! Living among these… these trailer park, orange picking, alligator wrestlers and flowery shirted, golf playing retirees who don't know how to vote. What kind of life can you possibly have here? who is there to… interact with who can possibly be your intellectual equal? I will tell: No one! Absolutely, no one!"

"I am perfectly happy here, Mother. I have plenty of friends; I have my own business…and now that I have Steve, I…"

Anne quickly interrupts Jan again.

"Steve? Not that deadbeat, daydreamer over there? Oh boy! And you call this a business? The only things missing here are pictures with clowns on them or some poker-playing dogs!"

Anne looks at another painting and then Sarcastically says, "This is a nice piece, I'm sure it'll end up in the lobby of a cheap little motel. I can already smell the room service on it. Can you honestly tell me that you can make a living selling this…This 'art'"?

"Yes, this place is doing okay; the gallery in Naples should break even this year, maybe show a little profit next year."

"Maybe, maybe!" Anne exclaims. "Oh please that's what you said last year. You've got to stop deluding yourself."

Just then Greg and Larry, a twenty-something college geek, enter with a big old beaten and battered backpack.

Larry speaks up first. "Hi, we've got a delivery for Jan, a

contract for her to review."

Linda watches him closely and says, "Sure. She's over there talking to her Mother. Jan, there's a delivery for you!" Linda yells across the floor.

Jan is grateful for the break in the conversation with her mother. "Thanks, Linda!"

Jan motions for Larry and Greg to walk to her. She sees a look of concern on Greg's face. Reassuring him, she continues to motion that they should join her. "Come on over, it's okay," Jan says.

When Greg and Larry reach where Jan is standing on the gallery floor with Anne, Jan says to Greg reassuringly, "Don't worry. You weren't interrupting anything important."

Greg and Larry walk over to Jan and Anne. Linda checks Larry out and likes what she sees. She licks her lips like a tiger settling on its next prey.

Larry turns around. Greg unzips the backpack, pulls out a pile of papers, handing them to Jan.

Larry is happy to be there and doesn't yet sense the tension between Anne and Jan. Greg speaks. "Here you go, as agreed - the full contract. Oh, hello. Don't believe I've had the pleasure."

Greg offers his hand to Anne, she ignores him. Greg drops his hand.

Jan leans forward and announces, "This is my mother, Anne Bentley. Who's your friend, Gregory?" Anne asks.

Jan shoots her mother a sharp look. She is shocked at her mother's forwardness. Anne whispers to Jan, "Just because I'm a happily married woman, doesn't mean I'm dead."

Greg turns to Larry, then to Jan, ignoring Anne... somewhat. "It's Greg, actually. Jan, this is Larry. He's a whiz with computers, and he's going to be setting up and running the website for us."

Jan shakes Larry's hand absent-mindedly. Anne has placed her hand on her chin, admiring Larry...

"Larry, good to meet you.

Wow, so, you guys must be doing pretty good - if you can afford to hire a staff."

"Actually," Larry begins, "they didn't. I heard about the company from my Dad - he's investing - and we worked out a little deal."

"Yeah, Larry works for us in exchange for a share in the company," Greg says.

"Ah, very good," Jan says without much thought.

Linda walks in with her eyes on solely on Larry. "Can I get you guys some coffee or something?"

Greg and Larry nod.

Larry can't stop staring at Linda and says, "Thanks. I like it with cream and four sugars."

Greg notices that Linda has not looked away from Larry. Nor Larry from Linda.

"Sure! Just black for me...Thanks." Greg calls after Linda. Linda has already walked away.

Linda goes to the coffee, watching Larry the whole time. She doesn't pay attention to what she's doing, so she puts way too much sugar in the coffee.

Frustrated by being ignored Anne muscles her way back into the conversation with a grunt and then, "Which one of you boys is Steve? Or is he still sleeping in? And, did I hear you say something about a new company?"

Greg steps forward. "I'm Greg, he's Larry and Steve is working on our project. Been up for hours. We're just preparing to launch it, and we've got investors all lined up."

Anne tries to be interested in the business side of the little circus in Jan's office. "I see. So, are you gentlemen doing an IPO?"

"What's that?" Asks Larry, as a blank look envelops his face.

"Initial Public Offering. Yes, ma'am," begins Greg. "Although not on the Exchange. My partner and I have about twenty investors in our new internet marketing company.

Anne feigns interest again. "Oh, it's merely a local company, is that it?"

Greg suspects Anne may be fishing for information out of him, not realizing she really doesn't care about their startup. He tries to answer cautiously. "Ah... yeah, but it's an internet firm. So, when you're doing that, THE WORLD is local!"

Anne gives another grunt. Linda is heading back over to the group. She presents Larry with a cup of coffee. Greg looks down at his hands, baffled, and wondering here *his* coffee is. Larry and Linda are the only two in existence as far as their stares are concerned. Larry gives Linda a big smile. Larry takes a tip of the coffee and almost gags on how sweet it is, but he manages to cover well. Anne gets to her feet. She suddenly announces her departure.

Anne suddenly announces her departure. "Well, I shall be running along, Janice. I have an important meeting with a *real* company."

"Whatever, Mom... All right, unthanks for stopping by. It was interesting meeting with you as always," Jan says, staring at the ceiling, trying to be calm, and not too sarcastic.

"Yes, Janice. I hope we don't do it again – very unsoon," Anne answers, mocking Jan. Anne marches out of the art gallery.

Greg stands silent for a moment until Anne has left the building. "Good God, woman. Was that really your mother? I mean, wow. She's quite the...interesting lady."

Jan let's the 'front' drop with her tensed shoulders. "She's a complete and total bitch, Greg. You can go ahead and call her that, no worries."

"Oh. Ah - I see. Well... I just didn't want to..." Greg lets his thoughts go unspoken.

"Insult her?" Jan asks.

"Yeah," Greg confirms.

Larry finally picks up on the tension that has left the room and says, "Why the totally negative energy in her aura, man? Doesn't she know that shit is bad for her karma?"

"As far as my mother is concerned, so long as something is good for her bank account - it's good!"

Greg's eyes begin to sparkle...with dollar signs. "Oh, a woman of... means, eh? You sure we can't get her to invest in our company?"

"Forget it, Greg. She's old money, which means she won't part with a penny unless it's an absolute sure thing."

"Really? Well, too bad I can't interest her in our little venture."

"Let me put it this way, if she ever goes broke, it means

the whole country has gone under!"

"Huh. I see." Greg seems disturbed.

"Ah... anyway, we should run along; got to meet with Steve on some... things."

Larry and Greg head for the front door. Linda gives Larry a big smile and leans forward in her chair, giving him quite the view down her blouse.

"Bye, Larry!" She says flirtatiously. Larry smiles at Linda with a bewildered look on his face. He keeps the image of Linda's blouse, or slight lack thereof in his mind. He is practically grinning from ear to ear, as he and Greg exit the art gallery. Greg knows the look – he's looked like a Cheshire cat before, too.

"Huh, now, just what was that all about? Jan asks. Yo, Linda, you want to slip 'em back in their sockets, and rein in the 'twins'"?

Linda sits back in her chair.

"Hey, just looking to...get me some too. And, hey... sometimes the twins get hungry."

Jan rolls her eyes, and shakes her head. "Wow. Too. Much. Information. On second thought, if you want to help Larry get some mud for his turtle, I've got no problem with that - just don't...be so OBVIOUS."

"Yes, milady." Linda says, grinning, mischievously.

Inside Steve's apartment, Larry sits at the table and works on his laptop, and Greg and Steve stand next to it.

Larry sits at the table and works on his laptop. Greg and Steve stand on either of side of Larry.

"So you finally nailed Jessica, you dog," says Steve, trying to be one of the guys without much confidence.

"Yup, and I've got the bruises around my waist to prove it." Greg announces proudly. "That girl has got some leg muscles. I hope she never wants oral sex; she'll get too excited and snap my neck in an instant."

Steve thinks about this for a moment and then, "Yeah, but, what a way to go; you got to admit. But, that shit-eating grin on your face tells me there's more to your glee than mere sex. Come on, man. Out with it."

"You know me so well." Greg begins to laugh and then turns serious. "It's money, my main man, big-big money. I ran into Jan's mother at her gallery today. She's in town for some sort of meeting, and I learned that she comes from old money, which means big-big-big money!"

"Huh, why? What, she's rich? Just her Mom or... the whole family?" Steve asks.

"Well, definitely her Mom. As for Jan, I'm not sure. The house I showed her wasn't all that fancy, but she did make a huge down payment. So, maybe she's got some decent money of her own. Didn't you know? Didn't Jan tell you?" Greg asks.

"Well... No, we never really talked about money. So, is her mother going to invest?" Steve replies.

"No - not yet. When I tried to give her my pitch, she cut me off. Seems she looks down her nose at start-up companies."

"Well, so, where does that leave us? If she shot you down already, what can we-?"

"We got to do an end-run on her. We just got to wine and dine Jan a bit, and then we use her to get to her mother -

and her mother's money. How about we line up something for all of us, tomorrow?" suggests Greg.

"Ah...you want me to come along? I don't...know about that one," Steve replies, hesitancy in his voice.

"Why, what's wrong?" Greg asks.

"Well...we had a...thing," says Steve, looking down at his feet.

"Yeah, I know," Greg answers.

"Huh - what - how?" Steve asks, shocked.

"I called you this morning, and Jan answered your pants."

"Oy!" Steve is not pleased by Greg's discovery.

"So what," Greg says. "It's not like it's true love, is it?"

"Ah...nooo," Steve replies.

"Then it's no big deal. Come on, Steve. Work with me here. It's simple, we connect with Jan, win her over, and then get her to bring in her Mother," Greg starts, grinning at his genius idea. "After that, you can dump her, and we get the money we need."

"God, ending up with Jan and her Mother? Sounds like a really weird double date. No, I can't do it. Not to Jan," Steve responds.

Larry laughs as Greg cringes.

"Ewww, Steve. Please don't joke about that!" Greg says. "Although, I got to say, her Mom's not half bad looking. If I didn't already have 'Anne Hathaway', I wouldn't mind going after 'Meryl Streep'. So, what do you say, my man; you ready to give your all to the 'Jan Project'"?

"Ah, Greg. You and your movie references. Sure, no prob'. You ready to get started, Larry?" Steve asked, patting

50

Larry on the back. Larry nods – he is excited at the thought of getting closer to Linda. Steve whips out his iPhone and makes some quick notes in it.

Larry wraps up his computer work. "Yeah OK, let's hit it! I've got all the new codes ready to upload to the website."

Not to be outdone, Greg whips out his cell phone and says, "Great, I'll put things in motion right now!"

Inside Jan's art gallery, a phone rings. Jan answers the phone on the second ring.

"Bentley Gallery. This is Jan. How may I assist you?"

"Hey, Jan, it's Greg," Greg says eagerly.

"Hey, Greg, what's up?" Jan replies.

"We've got some things to go over with you regarding the company. So, we'd like to take you to lunch tomorrow," Greg says.

"Ah... Do you really need to talk to me some more? After all, it's all just boring business stuff, and I've already invested," Jan replies, preoccupation in her voice.

"Well...I wanted to point out to you the enormous earning potential of our company, and that way you can speak about it to other potential investors. Ah...Larry is going to be there, and he wanted to ask Linda to come, but he was shy about it. Having you there would... smooth things over, okay?"

Larry does a double take and looks at Greg as if he's out of his mind.

"Ah...okay. You want me to mention it to Linda?"

"Sure, that'd make him feel much better."

"Okay, I'll do it."

Fleming's Steakhouse is a very nice, very fancy restaurant

with a small parking lot next to it and valet parking. Greg drives up in his simple car, parks and gets out. He opens the front passenger door and Jan gets out. Steve, Larry and Linda get out of the back passenger seats.

The interiors are quite the ritzy, clearly a very posh and expensive restaurant. Beautiful tables and chairs dot the main dining hall, and a fine reception area sits just inside the front door.

Greg, Steve, Larry, Linda and Jan enter, and are shown to a good table. Steve has his laptop, and he looks a bit nervous. Greg just about screams confidence.

Linda sits next to Larry, and is all smiles. Larry is quite happy, yet looks a bit nervous.

"Okay," Greg begins. "We will show you that, with a bit more investment, we could get the website expanded even further. Steve, show her the outline."

After dinner, Steve, now much more confident and animated, talks a blue steak to Jan. He sets up his laptop to show her his demo - and puts it in front of Larry and Linda, who only have eyes for each other. Jan watches intently.

Jan is not fully impressed. "Okay, I can see where this has major potential, but...I don't know that I can do much more."

"Oh, you don't have more money to invest?" Greg asks 'innocently'.

"No. What, you think I've got that kind of money?" Jan gestures at the chart on the computer screen.

"Not necessarily, but we thought your-I mean, you might know some people who did."

"Maybe. My Mother and the people she moves with, they could easily swing it, but..."

"What, you don't... get along with her?"

"Guys, I... hate to... air dirty laundry - family dirty laundry, but I guess I have to. My Mom pretty much cut me off when I left New York - and didn't marry the man she thought I should. So...I have pretty much cut her - and her money – off, too. It's like I was telling you, Steve, I believe in building up myself on my own - like my Dad taught me. So, what I got, I earned."

"Oh - so - you wouldn't be able to... convince her to make an investment in our company?"

"Naw, I doubt it. Sorry."

Steve pulls out his iPhone, making further notes. Jan sees the screen and sees a note labeled: "Jan Project". Clearly upset, she quickly covers up her anger, and maintains her composure.

"Well, no harm, no foul. Hey, if nothing else, now you know a lot more about us, and what we can do for our clients."

"Yeah, I know...plenty."

Outside Fleming's Steak House a valet drives up with Greg's car as Greg, Steve, Larry, Linda and Jan wait. Greg gives him a tip and gets in. Larry and Linda, still deep in conversation, get in the back, as does Jan. Steve gets in the front.

Greg drives along.

"Well," begins Linda, "I don't know about the rest of you, but I had a great time. I think your website has some real potential, Larry. Wish I had some money to invest in it," Linda says.

"You never know, Linda. Remember the dot.com bubble of the 90's," Jan says.

"So, what, now you're unsure about what we're doing?" Greg says, looking at Jan through the rearview mirror.

"Not at all. I'm just... cautious about getting deeply involved in... anything!" Jan replies.

"Very smart of you. You never know where something might lead," Steve says.

"Yeah, so I've learned."

Greg speaks up and asks, "Shall I drop you ladies back at the gallery?"

"Yes, thanks." Jan says casually.

"Ah... do we-?" Protests Linda.

Jan shoots Linda an icy stare.

"Yeah - right. Art Gallery, please," Linda says, quickly.

Once Jan and Linda are back at the art gallery, Jan storms in and rushes by Linda's desk. Just about blowing the papers off its surface. Linda follows, and acts as if she's caught up in the whirlwind of a hurricane that has just torn by.

"Whoa, Jan. You wanna keep it under 55? God, talk about earning yourself a speeding ticket?" Linda says, her eyes following Jan.

Jan storms into her office a wipes away a tear. Linda very cautiously looks in the door.

Linda looks perplexed and asks, "Ah...Is it safe for me to...come in?"

"Yeah - sure, sorry, Linda. I'm not mad at you," Jan says as Linda enters.

"Well, that was just about the biggest brush off in history!"

"Huh...What are you talking about?"

"They're just after my mom's money…. And they're trying to go through me to get it!" Jan says, on the verge of tears.

"Well, but, Jan, you did say that Steve was just a fling. So, what's the big deal?"

"That's true… It's just… Steve had something in his iPhone about the "Jan Project" - like I was just some sort of business proposition! So, did he not even care about me? Was I not even a decent lay…was I just work to him? God, talk about making me feel cheap and used?"

Linda watches Jan cover her face with her hands. "Why don't we go out tonight? Come with me to that little club I told you about. It's a really great release and I-"

"No thanks, Linda. No offense, but I prefer a club where handcuffs are not considered an accessory," says Jan.

"Don't knock it 'til you've tried it. What consenting adults do in private is their business," Linda adds.

"I don't have a problem with that. I just don't care to be one of the adults. A little slap and tickle with Steve was fine, but your friends play too rough. I'll be fine; I've got some friends online that I can chat with, and take my mind off of… things," Jan responds.

"Have you had cybersex with any of them yet?" Linda asks, seriously.

"Linda, why this constant preoccupation with sex?" Jan asks, rhetorically.

"Lack of occupation with sex. I'm going for a new record here, I may recover my virginity," Linda says jokingly.

Jan cannot believe her ears. "Well, what about your club friends, don't you-?"

"Jan! That's 'recreation'. There's no sex involved; the police would bust the place."

"Ah, I see." Jan stares at Linda, confused and then flips through some papers on her desk, trying to look in control of life.

"Actually, Linda, you know what? I think I may go out of town," Jan says, jumping to her feet.

"Huh, just to... avoid Steve? Isn't that a bit much?" Linda cautions.

"It isn't so much about getting away from him as giving me some breathing room. The big art festival is coming up in Naples next week. It's a perfect time for me to go down, check out the other store, and look for some new pieces," Jan says, starting to feel somewhat back in control.

"Okay. So... you want me to handle things here?" Linda asks.

"You up for it?" Jan smiles.

"You got it!" Linda smiles back.

"Okay. I'll come in tomorrow morning, take care of a few things, and then take off. After that - the place is all yours. Try not to burn it down while I'm gone, please"

Jan and Linda laugh. They both suddenly turn around, hearing a voice from the front of the gallery.

"Hello-hello," Larry says raising his voice a little. "Anyone here? Linda, I'm here!" Linda jumps to her feet and runs out. Jan follows. Linda and Larry are at Linda's desk, locked in an embrace. Larry has his backpack. Jan walks up to them.

Jan finally speaks up. "Larry, what are you doing here, did Steve send you. I...?"

"I'm picking up Linda; we're going out tonight," Larry says, with a grin.

"Really?" Jan says, looking at Linda, sharply.

"Yeah," Larry begins to explain. "We set it up over lunch."

Linda is very excited to be standing so close to Larry. She cannot contain the excitement in her voice. "So, 'Boss Lady'…is it okay if I take off?"

"Sure, go ahead. I'll lock up the place," Jan says, ushering the two lovebirds out of the art gallery.

"Thank you, thank you, milady; a thousand blessings on you and your household," Linda says, looking over her shoulder as she's ushered out.

"Very funny…thanks," Jan replies.

Larry looks at Linda and says casually, "I brought all the stuff you wanted, Linda, but what do we need a hairbrush for?"

Larry swings his backpack around to the front of his chest. He tries to stop, so he can open it; look for something. Linda stops him, and pushes him out the door.

"Never mind that now, Larry, I'll show you later," Linda starts.

Linda turns to Jan, grinning and says,

"I'm feeling so very, very bad tonight!"

"I don't want to know!" Jan shouts with her hands up. "Have fun… ah, don't do anything I wouldn't… ah, oh screw it, and just don't get busted."

The sun hangs low in the sky as Greg sits behind the wheel and drives along with Steve.

"Ah, Greg? Where are we going now? This isn't the way

to get to my apartment," Steve asks.

"Not to worry, my man. We are making a slight detour. Does the name Hillary James mean anything to you?" Greg asks Steve.

"Ah... no, should it? Wait, it is...sounds somewhat familiar," Steve replies.

"Number one, she's one of our investors, and two, she's a local publisher. She's asked us to come by her office for a little one-on-one meeting. Well, I guess I should say two-on-one," Greg says, counting the reasons on his hand.

"Oh - yes, now I remember. Yeah, I met her at that presentation we did at Jan's gallery. Yeah, she seemed very nice. So, what, we're meeting with her right now? Sheesh, Greg, I just spent all afternoon spinning our tale to-" Steve responds, slightly perturbed at the time wasted.

"Steve, you got to strike while the iron is hot! Not only can Miss James invest more money in our site, think of the promotional efforts she can do for us through her company. It's not enough to have a better "mousetrap," the world has to know about it."

"Oh...okay." Steve says. "Look, when we get a little more money in our pockets. Can we afford something nice in the way of, say...a car?"

Steve begins to daydream again and his mind wanders into a large building with a huge parking lot in front of it. It's full of many very expensive cars.

Steve looks over several expensive cars: BMW, Rolls Royce, etc. and points to all of them. The car dealer smiles and starts to write up some paperwork.

"Some excellent choices, sir," says the dealer. "Now, if

you'll just sign here?"

Steve moves to look at the paperwork and picks up a pen.

"Sure, I…" Steve begins to read the fine print of the deal. "Whoa, they're going to cost me how much?"

"Well," begins the dealer, cranking up his charm, "you're paying for the best, sir. Oh, and let's not forget the taxes, tags, and auto insurance; you'll need all that too."

"Oy, maybe I should stick to something simpler."

Greg, dressed as a driver, pulls up in a very long limo.

The dealer step toward the limo and waves a hand in the air like a game show hostess showing off the prize package and says, "Is this more what you were thinking of, sir?"

Steve smiles and begins to laugh.

"Oh yeah!"

The back seat area inside the long limo has seats, a TV, DVD player, radio, and a full bar.

Steve climbs in, sits in back and fixes himself a drink as Greg drives. Greg zips around a corner; Steve falls to the floor, spilling his drink.

"Easy there, Greg!" Steve shouts, trying not to spill his drink again.

Steve tries to get some ice, but Greg makes another sharp turn, and the ice goes everywhere. Steve tries to get to his feet; he slips and slides all over the place. He reaches out, grabs a door handle, and accidentally opens it.

The WIND howls through the interior - papers, magazines and all manner of things go every which way. A tumbleweed blows by in front of Steve's face. He struggles with the door, slips on the ice cubes, and tumbles out of the door and back to reality.

"Huh, I think I better remember to wear my seatbelt," Steve says.

"Huh, what?" Greg asks.

"Nothing." Steve shakes his head.

Greg pulls up to a nice office building in the downtown area. They pull into a parking garage and park. Hillary's office is sleek and elegant with a bookcase full of leather-bound books.

Hillary sits behind the desk and flips through a file. Steve sits in front of her desk, as Greg stands off to the side. Steve looks very nervous. Greg looks very calm.

"Well, I must say, Steve, Greg, I think this website of yours, the "Idea Marketplace," Stevenetwork.com has enormous potential!"

Greg gives a slight bow and says, "Why, thank you, Miss James; we think so too."

"Ah, but do you see its true potential? One thing I've learned from the writing and publishing business is this, one word – networking," Hillary says.

"Networking? Ah... how does that factor into-," Greg asks.

"Ah, I see what you mean," Steve begins, "bringing people together who have something in common, whether it's a writer who's good at sci-fi and someone with an idea for a book or..."

A laughing, Hillary says, "Yes, or someone with an idea for a new 'widget', and the people he needs to connect with in order to make it happen. You're very fast at picking up on things, Steve – I like that in a man."

"So... just what are you suggesting we do?" Greg asks.

Steve's face lights up. "I see it; we expand our website. It won't just be a place for people to post their ideas, we'll also help them to network with the sorts of people who'll want to invest and/or promote their idea!"

Hillary is impressed. She smiles at Steve. "Once again, you're on top of things, Steve – another attribute I like in a man."

"Ah...Thanks."

Perplexed and a little jealous at being left out of the conversation, Greg interrupts. "Huh, and it would only require a slight modification to the website. Miss James, you are a certified genius!"

"Oh, I'm just a woman who knows what she wants, and how to get it. Tell you what, why don't we go to dinner and discuss some other ideas I have, Steve? You like steak? Fleming's serves the best in town."

"Fleming's? Ah…"

"He'll be happy to." Greg announces.

"Greg!" Steve says quickly.

"Wonderful!" Hillary gets to her feet and moves to get her coat and briefcase.

"Ah...well...what about Greg? Shouldn't he-?" Steve asks.

"Steve, you need to learn, I'm a woman who knows what she wants, and I get it! Right now, I want you."

"She's right, Steve; there's no need for both of us to be there. Go, have fun, enjoy yourself."

"Ah…okay," Steve says, rising from the chair.

Hillary takes Steve's arm, leading him toward the door. Steve looks to Greg, who gives him a big smile and a thumb's up.

Hillary pulls up to the valet parking in her BMW at Fleming's restaurant. She gets out with her briefcase, hands the keys to the valet, and Steve comes around to take her hand. The Valet does a double take when he sees Steve, and looks at the other valets waiting by the door. They all watch Steve go in, and shrug.

Hillary and Steve are shown to the best table in the house. All of the STAFF are surprised to see Steve there again, but they cover it well.

Hillary orders for both of them, which clearly surprises Steve - he never even gets to see a menu - then she grabs her briefcase, puts it on the table, and opens it.

"All right, let's go over a few of my ideas for the website, and the company." Hillary says quickly.

"Sure. Of course, I'll have to run all of your ideas by Greg. You understand?" Steve asks to clarify the terms of the agreement.

"Oh, certainly-certainly. Sorry, Steve, if I come on a little strong, but when you're a woman in what is still essentially a man's world, you learn to "grow a pair" real fast!"

"Ah... I see. Well, in dealing with Greg and me, you'll always get a fair deal. And, come to think of it, why did you only want to meet with me? I mean, after all, Greg and I are partners."

"Partners in business; not partners in life."

"Huh?" Steve says, confused. Hillary takes Steve's hand in hers.

"I wanted to get to know you better, Steve, and not in a business sense; in a... biblical sense!"

"Sorry, Hillary, I'm not up on my Bible."

Hillary sighs. "Oh, my boy, are you really so innocent?"

Steve gives Hillary a blank look. She smiles.

"I guess you truly are. Ah, that's so sweet." She says just a little disappointed.

Over the next few hours, Hillary and Steve have dinner. Steve takes steps to avoid eating too much - as he's full from lunch. So, he goes to great lengths to hide his food all over the place. He slips food under the table, puts it on the trays of passing waiters, and even uses his fork to launch chunks of meat across the room.

"Can I leave the tip?" Steve asks.

"I hate to think that I'm not contributing anything to the-"

"Now-now, Steve, this is my party. Come on, coffee and dessert at my place."

"Dessert? Oh, I don't know that I could eat any more!"

"You haven't seen what I'll be... serving."

"Ah... Okay."

Steve begins to daydream again.

He imagines a large room with a wooden post at the center and many implements of torture hanging on the walls: whips, canes, paddles, and so on.

Steve stands chained to a post, naked except for his boxers. Hillary stands behind him in the classic dominatrix outfit: hip boots with six-inch heels, a tight corset and studded collar. She holds a long whip.

"Now, slave," Hillary says in a dominant voice, "you will learn to obey your mistress."

Hillary cracks the whip. Steve swallows hard and closes his eyes. Slowly his mind returns to the restaurant.

"I hope your...dessert isn't too... stingy; I happen to have a sensitive... Stomach." He says. Hillary and Steve leave Fleming's, and head to Hillary's house.

Hillary's home is a large and very fancy home in an upscale neighborhood. Both its lawn and garden are perfect - a wrought-iron fence and gate surround it.

Hillary drives up to the gate, it swings open, and she drives in. Steve looks out at the house and grounds, totally in awe. One of the doors of the three-car garage opens, and Hillary drives in.

Hillary leads him through the house and upstairs to a very nice room, beautifully decorated, and with a huge bed. Hillary slowly undresses Steve and pushes him onto the bed.

Sitting on the side of the bed naked, Steve looks uncomfortable, but ready for her as she puts a little ladies nightcap on his head.

"Okay, you just sit there while I slip into...my outfit, and I'll be right back," Hillary says, not able to contain her excitement.

"Ah...okay. But, what's with the hat?"

"You'll understand when you see my outfit. Okay?" She says.

Steve swallows hard. Hillary heads for a door, and exits the room.

"Hmm...Okay." Steve sits, scanning the room. There are

many photos of Hillary showing some of the events of her life: college, skydiving, scuba diving, hand gliding, and so on. It's clear from the pictures that she enjoys life to the fullest, and with many people.

Hillary enters, dressed as Red Riding Hood - complete with a basket of goodies. She comes over to sit on the edge of the bed and gives Steve an innocent look.

"Hello, Grandpa. Why, what big eyes you have?"

Steve is amazed at how Hillary looks, and that she has an active fantasy life.

"Ah... All the better to see you, my dear," Steve says, struggling to remember the old story while staring at Hillary's body.

"And, Grandpa, what very big ears you have?" Hillary says, leaning in.

"All the better to hear you with, my dear." Steve now has a great view of her leaning into him.

"And, Grandpa, what big teeth you have?"

"Ah...all the better to...eat you with, my dear!" Steve says almost salivating.

Hillary stands up straight and drops the basket on the bed; inside it are various sex toys.

"Eat me? Well, guess I won't need these clothes, then," Hillary says, pulling the string of her hood. Her entire outfit falls away, and she stands there naked. Steve's eyes grow wide as he takes in the sight of Hillary. "Let's eat," Hillary announces, diving into bed.

Hillary and Steve make furious love in bed. Then, Hillary is dressed as a Catholic schoolgirl, lying across Steve's lap as he sits in a chair, and he spanks her. Then, Hillary is in a lion costume and Steve is dressed as a lion tamer. He tries to keep Hillary at bay, but she leaps at him, knocks him back onto the bed, and they continue having sex.

Hillary and Steve lay in bed, in each other's arms. All around them are all various sorts of costumes and sex toys.

"Holy shit," Steve exclaims. "I'm so dehydrated; I may dry up, turn to dust, and blow away!"

Hillary begins to laugh. "What's wrong, baby, I drain you of all your...bodily fluids? You need to...reload?"

"Just about! God, you got some... stamina, Hill'," Steve says, panting.

"Ah-ah, Steve, please - Hillary. Hill' is only for the schoolgirl fantasy. Got it?" Hillary says.

"Ah...Okay. Sorry, it's going to take me a while to get all the... roles right," Steve says, apologizing.

"I could always... punish you, for forgetting!" Hillary says, with a wink in her voice.

"Ah... no thanks. I'm not into that sort of stuff," Steve responds, swallowing hard.

"Okay, sure, no problem. Not everyone is into it, and I respect your feelings." She pauses for a moment and then asks, "Ah, are you okay with me being into it?"

"Sure; I'm always open to... new things," says Steve. Hillary laughs, reaching back to rub her behind.

"I thought so; you sure didn't need much encouragement to...give me... what I like!" Another flirtatious wink in her voice.

"Well, I aim to please, my dear. I aim to please," says

Steve, flirtatiously.

Hillary embraces Steve; they kiss and start to make love again.

"My kind of man! You know, Steve. This may not be the best time to mention it, but I'm the sort of person who likes to strike while the iron is hot," Hillary announces.

"Mention what? You haven't got some other...things you want to do? Unless you've got a double dose of Viagra, I don't think I can... deliver much more," says Steve.

"No, no," she says laughing. "You've got a ton of stories about successful ways of making money, and ones that don't work. Anyone looking to make money - anyone who wants to make a million - would love to read about that. I'm thinking, it's got real potential; you should write a book, and then I'll publish it," Hillary says.

"Really, a book? Wow, that's a great idea!" Steve is surprised, though pleased at the idea.

Steve rolls out of bed so fast that Hillary is caught by surprise. He jumps to his feet and moves to a nearby desk, feet landing on the floor.

"Slow down, tiger. I'll have a contract drawn up tomorrow, and we can sign everything right and proper."

"Oh - okay. Ah...Sorry, I was just excited about getting started."

Hillary looks at her watch.

"Yes, I know, you're just full of excitement over...all kinds of things."

"Thanks for understanding. You got paper somewhere?"

"Living room. Why don't we-?" Hillary starts.

"Thanks," Steve says, bolting for the door. He exits the room. Hillary gets to her feet. "Yeah, full of excitement, alright. Ah, gotta love that boy!"

Meanwhile, at Jan's gallery, Linda sits at her desk; she has a large pillow on her chair, and a devilish grin on her face. Jan enters.

"Oh boy, I know that look. You "got some" last night didn't you, Linda?"

"That I did, and it was as good as I remember. Larry may not be the sharpest tool in the shed, but he learns quickly, and boy, he gave me the best-"

"Linda, please. T.M.I. I don't want any details. Any calls?"

Jan heads for her office. Linda rises, following Jan, quickly.

"No, but your Mother…" Linda begins.

"Called again? I'll, just…" Jan says absent-mindedly.

Jan opens her office door as she looks toward Linda. Jan looks in. Anne sits there. Linda comes up next to Jan in the door.

"No, she's waiting for you in your office. That's what I was trying to tell you," Linda calls out.

"Ah, Janice, there you are, my dear – finally," Anne says.

Coldly, Jan turns to Linda.

"Thanks. Why don't you make us some coffee?"

"Sure, why not? I prefer standing up now anyway," Linda tries to avoid Jan's stare. She heads out to make the coffee. Jan reluctantly enters her office, taking a seat behind the desk in front of her Mother.

"What is it this time, Mother? Another merger? Hostile takeover? Leveraged buyout?"

"No business this time, dear. I'm on my way to the airport for a little fun. You're looking well. The Florida sun doesn't seem to be drying out your skin too much."

"Thanks," She says with sarcasm. "You look good too; those Botox shots are really helping."

"Thank you." Anne is happy, unfazed. "I had a treatment right before I left New York; want to look my best on vacation."

"Well... that's... good." Jan says not knowing what to expect next from her mother.

"Yes. Anyway, I'm off now, going to take a little vacation. I'll be back in a few months on my way to-"

"Months?" Jan asks.

"Yes. Months. I'm taking a trip around the world, Janice. So, it'll be a while before I get back. Anyway, I'll have a layover here. I was thinking perhaps you could join me on the final leg back to New York," Anne finishes.

"I'll think about it, Mother," Jan answers.

"Thank you, Janice. I have to run along, my flight leaves soon and I have to find my way back to what passes for an airport in this silly town," Anne replies.

They both rise from their chairs, heading towards Jan's office door.

Don't knock it, Mother. It used to be a lot smaller "B.D." "

"What?" Anne asks, perplexed.

"Before Disney," Jan replies.

"Of course. His parks may be tacky, but his movies were always nice, not full of sex and violence. Good-bye, Janice," Anne says.

They reach the front door.

"Bye, Mom."

At the door, they give each other a small, posh hug. Anne makes her way to the art gallery's exit, slowly walking past Linda and the waiting coffee. Jan walks back toward her office. Linda stands at her desk.

"Boy, I can feel the love rolling off you two, when I see something like that." Linda says, sarcastically.

"Hey, for my Mom, that's a breakthrough. She's invited me to come home for a little visit - and she was actually very civil about the whole thing. So, maybe…" Jan trails off.

"Damn, I miss all the good stuff! If you guys had been as loud as you were last time, I would have heard all that." Linda laughs. Jan joins her.

"Very funny," Jan says, regaining her composure.

"So, you going to do it, pop on up to the Big Apple?"

"Maybe. I'd sure love to see my brother and sister, and all my old friends again."

"Now, you're talking. That's what you need to perk yourself up and get over Steve, a little action downtown." Linda says, looking at Jan's crotch. "Did wonders for the state of my mental health."

Jan shakes her head. "Yeah. Still, one thing at a time; I'll get ready for my trip, and think about "Mommy Dearest" later. Funny the way different events come together all at once like that."

"Well, sometimes the weirdest, most random events can come together and produce the most unexpected of results," Linda exclaims.

"Where the Hell did you get that line of bull?" Jan asks, hands on hips.

"My boyfriend Larry, he's a math major at UCF. He was explaining 'Chaos Theory' to me late last night, while I was lying across his lap and he was-"

"TMI. T…M…I… That's more information than I need to know, period. And, thank you so much for that almost eye-searing visual," Jan starts. "And…by the way, I do not need to 'get over' Steve. There is and was nothing to 'get over' from. Like I told you, it was a one-night stand. It didn't mean a thing. I'm totally over him, cool?"

Jan turns, making her way back into her office.

"Yeah, okay Lighten up, Jan. I believe you. As for my fun, don't knock it 'til you try it, I always say. It's a lifestyle choice!"

Linda grins and sits down gingerly on her pillow. Jan goes into her office. Linda takes out a leather whip from her desk, looking at it longingly.

Linda holds the whip firmly and asks an absent Jan, "The question is - do you believe it? Sounds to me like you got it bad for Stevie boy."

Back in Steve's apartment, Greg sits on the couch and Steve is at his desk, both have their iPads open.

"Okay, that takes care of the changes Larry has made to the website. Stevenetwork.com. The 'Idea Marketplace' is fully up and running. Already, we've seen some major projects get posted," Greg says.

"Good, good. What about the office space, how's that going? Want some more coffee?"

Steve crosses the living room to the kitchen. Once there, he pours a cup.

"No thanks," Greg starts. "I prefer coffee you don't have to chew. I found two places. One's up on Lee Road, the other is down on South Street. Both have good square footage, easy access to I-4 and they can handle our electronic needs."

Steve leaves the kitchen; crosses the living room to his desk; and, sits down.

"Good. Set up a meeting with the owners. Anything else?" Steve asks.

"Got a call from Dwight. Says he's desperate to get some help with his latest catering job. He says he could use your help...," Greg trails off.

Steve begins to laugh. "This from the man who said that he wouldn't hire me again - no matter what?"

"Yeah, yours truly...one and the same." Greg snorts.

"Oh... I don't know. I don't think I don't think I'll need his jobs anymore," Steve says with confidence.

"True, but, I thought I should at least mention it to you," says Greg, reassuring his friend.

"Thanks, but I'm thinking I'll pass on his jobs. I will give him a call and see how he's going, though. I mean, after all, we're still buddies."

"Okay, that's that At least for the website. Now, what about this book project? I think it's an awesome idea; you start on it yet?" asks Greg.

"Greg, for Pete's sake, Hill' - I mean - Hillary only suggested it last night!"

Greg moves to the desk, picks up a pile of papers and flips through them.

"Yeah, and you've already written this much. So, that tells

me that you're really inspired. So, how is it going?" Greg smirks.

"So... Okay, yes, I've written up a few notes. It's going to take a while, okay?" Steve quickly answers.

"Okay, I get it." Greg rubs the back of his neck. "Man, is my neck killing me! I swear I need a message!"

"What's the matter?" Steve asks, concerned.

"Ah...Date with Jessica last night and...overdid it."

Greg quickly changes the subject of the conversation. "Anyway, two things on the fun front. Jessie and I, and Larry and Linda are going out tonight. Jessie has a friend, care to join us? I'm thinking that you could use the break."

"No thanks; I want to keep working on the book, and I want to get together with Jan." Steve says casually.

Greg cannot believe his ears. "Jan? Oh, I thought our 'Lady Publisher' was now your 'flavor of the month'?"

That was just a... fling. She just wanted a bit of fun. I...I have real...real feelings for Jan, and I want to...to be with her." Steve is sincere, and struggles to come out with the right words.

"Okay, man, your choice. Number two, the theater's doing "Kiss Me, Kate" in the fall. You want to reserve some tickets and we go see it?" asks Greg.

"Oh, I don't know. I'm not much for the theater. Why do you ask, is Jessie going to be in it?" Steve replies.

"No, but get this - Linda talked Larry into trying out. The two of them are playing the leads!" Greg exclaims.

"Larry? Our Larry has the lead? Oh, I got to see this show, just to see that. How'd he ever manage to get that part?"

Steve is bewildered.

"Said it was Linda's influence. Said they prepared for the audition for weeks, and have been busting ass every night getting ready for opening night," Greg says, playing with a booger he just dug out of his nose, rolling it around with his thumb and index fingers into a little ball, and flicking it somewhere across Steve's living room. It's small, but he hears it land. TAP!

"Wow, they're rehearsing this far in advance? Boy, I bet it'll be great. Okay, I'm in," Greg tells Steve.

"Great. As it doesn't open for a couple months, you've got some time to work on the 'Hillary Project'," Greg suggests, winking at Steve and giving him the 'thumbs up' sign at the same time.

Steve begins to laugh. "Oh, Greg! You and your project names; everything with a label!"

"Hey, you got to keep your work organized! Now, you get to your writing, and I'll see about the office space, okay?"

"Deal."

Steve begins to daydream again. This time his mind concocts a mystical nightclub with a large parking lot.

On and off, a huge neon sign sits atop the building, flashing. The sign reads: Club Harem.

The parking lot is full. People move in and out of the club in large numbers. Inside there is a large open area filled with tables and chairs. A dance stage has curtains on either side and multiple poles spaced evenly across it.

Greg and Steve sit at a corner table, dressed very fancily and each with two scantily clad dancers next to them. On the stage, Hillary, Linda and Jan dance. The place is full of people.

"Yes, this is the life, my man! Looking good!" Greg shouts to Steve.

Steve and Greg toast one another with their champagne glasses as Jan and Linda gyrate on either side of Hillary.

"You got that right, dude. With a great club like this, we've got no worries," Steve announces to Greg.

The Dancers pop pills and snort drugs. Greg joins them, and Steve looks worried. Steve looks around. Men are offering money to Jan, Linda and the other dancers, and they're going off with them to private rooms in the back.

"Huh, I wonder what's going on back there?" Steve says.

Sirens blare. The door bursts open, ten S.W.A.T. team members rush in and start arresting people.

"THIS IS A RAID!" A policeman yells. "EVERYONE, ON THE GROUND, NOW! NOW! NOW! NOW!"

Outside, Greg, Steve and the others - all in handcuffs - are marched towards, and then loaded into an unmarked van. Local, national, and international News teams swarm around them taking pictures and video footage.

A reporter looks into a camera and says, "Local men running night club arrested for prostitution and drug sales; story at eleven."

The daydream ends.

Steve comes back to his senses and says, "Ah... okay, maybe we'll invest our money in something a bit less... Exciting."

Steve pulls together some notes, looks at his watch and grabs his iPhone. He dials.

Linda sits at her desk in Jan's gallery. Jan, bag in hand, heads out the door.

The phone rings and Linda answers it. "Hello, Bentley Gallery, can I help you?"

"Hey, Linda, it's Steve. Is Jan around now?"

"You just missed her, Steve."

"Oh? Rats! Okay, I'll catch her later; bye!"

"Oh, but she…" Linda begins to explain but Steve hangs up before Linda can finish her sentence.

Steve sits at his desk, furiously writing away on his laptop. He's been at this quite some time. The growth of hair on his face, and the ever-growing pile of dirty dishes, and crumpled up paper, shows just how much time has passed. He doesn't spend all of this time completely alone – Greg and Hillary come and go, separately. Finally, Steve sifts through a huge pile of papers - his full manuscript, and sighs. He also finds Greg's dried and shriveled up booger. 'Hmm. I knew I heard something; wondered where it went.' He thinks to himself.

Steve's fingers are killing him. Steve scratches his face - he's got three-days' worth of growth on it. He looks at the calendar on his desk.

"Wow, time sure does fly when you're having fun!" He says to himself.

Just then, Hillary, dressed as Little Bo Peep, comes out of the bedroom and walks over to him.

"You can say that again, my boy. So, how's it going?"

"Take a look; the book is finally done." Steve said anxiously.

"Yes, that's my boy! Oh, we need to go out and celebrate."

Hillary is really excited now.

"Ah... Okay, but you might want to change first," Steve suggests.

"Yeah, I guess so." Hillary said beginning to laugh.

Hillary turns to leave and change her clothes. She exits the room. Steve dials his phone, grimaces and yelps in pain as he pushes the buttons.

"Hey, Linda; it's Steve again. Is Jan around- what, still? Goodness, when is she coming back? Huh - I see. Well, no, no message." Steve hangs up.

Steve says to himself, "If she won't call me, I'm not calling her either!"

Hillary comes out of the bedroom, dressed nicely. She picks up the manuscript, stuffing it in her briefcase.

"All right lover," she says. "Let's get to it. One party coming up, and then I get this to the editor, and then - who knows?

"Yeah... who knows?" Steve has gone without sleep for days. His mind slips into another daydream.

The clear blue-green waters of the Atlantic. A few fluffy white clouds drift overhead.

Steve, decked out in full yachting garb, stands at the steering wheel of a huge luxury motor boat. Greg, Hillary, Linda, Larry and Jan - dressed for fun in the sun - recline in deck chairs.

Steve steers the boat. Many rocks and reefs appear in front of the boat like an obstacle course. Steve swerves to avoid them. The others are tossed about - they fall all over the place, spill their drinks and drop food on each other.

Steve Seven

The skies grow dark, the waves get larger, and soon a full hurricane is howling about them.

Steve slowly exits his daydream, and comes back to reality. "Huh, maybe I'll stick to... land-based stuff."

Over the next few hours and days reality sets in for Steve, as he and Hillary meet at her office to review the manuscript and contract.

Hillary, an editor and Steve look over the book, and make notes.

Steve talks on the phone to Linda several times, but she keeps telling him that Jan is not there.

Hillary presents Steve with the first copy of the book. They all congratulate each other for a job well done, as they look the book over.

With his book complete, Steve and Hillary travel to New York to sell it to the big publishers.

They arrive in the Big Apple, with an overview of the city with JFK Airport in the foreground.

A jet swoops low in the sky and lands on the tarmac.

They sit in the back of a taxi quietly as Steve ponders the height of the building. Hillary is very reserved, while Steve is like an excited kid. The taxi pulls up to The Plaza hotel. They get out; Hillary pays the tab and directs a bellhop to get their bags. She leads Steve inside.

Hillary moves to the desk and checks in. Steve stands and looks around, taking it all in. The Bellhop comes in with their bags, and the manager gives them a room key card. The Bellhop leads Hillary and Steve to the elevator. Steve whips out his iPhone and checks his email, but he has no messages. He frowns.

Along a wide and plush hall with expensive wall- to-wall carpeting and fancy lighting fixtures.

An elevator door opens. The Bellhop leads Steve and Hillary down the hall. Steve continues to play a game on his iPhone as they walk.

They come up to a door. The Bellhop swipes a key card, the lock flashes green, and he opens the door. He goes in, and Hillary and Steve follow.

Once inside their lavish room with a large king-sized bed and windows that look out over the city, Steve takes in the view of New York and whistles.

The Bellhop sets the bags down. Hillary gives him a tip, and he exits. Steve puts down his iPhone, picks up his laptop case and opens it. He sets the computer on a desk under the window and starts it up.

Hillary calls out, "Steve, what are you doing?"

Steve, not paying very much attention, answers quite absent-mindedly, "I just wanted to check on how the website is doing, before we go to the meeting."

"Go, where?"

"Ah...the publisher. Aren't we meeting with them?"

Hillary slips off her coat and sits on the bed. She begins to slowly unbutton her silk blouse, revealing a low cut, lace bra that leaves her nipples exposed. "Yes, but that's not until tomorrow." She says flirting. "We have time to...relax. And, they're not a publisher, dear; I'm the publisher. This company will help us to launch the book signing tour. They are experts at promotions."

Steve looks around, finally noticing Hillary caressing her left breast with the back of her hand.

"Ah, I get it. Hey now, this is some awesome room!" He says.

"Yes, it is, sweetie. Now, why not come to bed for a few hours of slap and tickle, and I'll relieve all your stress," says Hillary, suggestively and seductively.

"Huh - what? Oh... gee, Hillary, you're about as subtle as a slap in the face!" Steve exclaims.

"Not to worry, sweetie, I'll never do that - unless you ask for it!"

She grins and stands up, dropping her clothes to the floor. She stands there in her lace underwear, and Steve crosses to her. They embrace and kiss, and fall back on the bed. He starts to undress, and she helps him. Just then Steve's open laptop computer announces,

"You've got mail, Steve!"

Steve jumps out of bed, races to his laptop and checks his mail. Hillary practically falls out of bed. Hillary sits up frustrated by the interruption, hands folder in front of her chest.

"Oh wow, look at this, the promotion company sent us tickets to a show for tonight!" Steve is excited at this news.

Hillary is not excited about the news. She sits up. "Yeah - great - wonderful. Sweetie, I think you need to learn to prioritize better."

"Huh?" Steve turns around.

"Which is more important to you right now, Steve: getting your mail, or getting laid?" Hillary demands.

"Oh... Sorry." Steve tries to sound sincere.

"It's okay, my boy; you're forgiven – provided you give

Miss Hillary her "sugar".

Steve closes his laptop, and moves toward Hillary, as she gets to her feet. They both move to the bed. Hillary and Steve make love.

The following day, they sit together in a spacious room with a huge oval table and many fine chairs. A sideboard has coffee, tea, and donuts and bagels.

Steve and Hillary meet with a book agent and review a contract. Steve looks very happy. He signs the contract, and then gets a bunch of donuts and starts to eat.

"Well, I must say, Hillary," the agent begins, "it looks like you've snagged a real winner this time. If this book does as well as we expect, the two of you will make out like bandits!"

"Yes, it's not often you find a writer like Steve. The boy is quite...gifted, in so many ways. And, I'm not at all concerned about making money for me." Hillary says.

"Oh - really?" Asks the agent.

"I am more than comfortable, my friend. My dear husband, may he rest in peace, always believed that a person only needs a certain amount to live on. Beyond that is pure greed!" says Hillary, assertively.

This makes the agent uneasy and then says, "Ah, I see. Huh, a very wise man."

"Yeah, I do miss him," Hillary says, looking down slightly, and playing with her hands.

"Well, in that case, young Mister Lowe here is looking to make out quite well," say the Agent, confidently.

"Yes, I think so, and the dear boy deserves it; he is one hard worker, let me tell you," says Hillary, agreeing with the

Agent's statement.

"God, would you look at him load up on the sugar? You'd think he was going to run a marathon race, or something," the agent exclaims.

"Yes, my boy does definitely needs his energy for…. He sure is a hard worker…," says Hillary thinking of something else.

"Well, then I'll let you two get going. I've spoken to our people; we're ready to get started," says the Agent wrapping up the conversation, and rise from his seat.

"Excellent! I think we should kick it off back home. You know how the local press eats that sort of thing up; you know, the old "local boy makes good" sort of thing," replies Hillary, also rising from her seat, and moving toward the Agent, hand outstretched to shake his hand.

"You got it. We'll do the press release, line up some radio and TV spots and interviews, and get the ball rolling."

Hillary and the Agent shake each other's hand.

"Steve, it's time to get going. We have to put all that sugar to use."

Steve snags one more donut.

"Oh, okay." Steve pauses to chew. "So, what next?"

Back at the hotel room, Steve and Hillary make love.

There are clear blue skies over the U.S. eastern coast. A jet flies through the sky, heading south as the sun sets in the west. The duo are heading back home to Florida.

Back in Florida, we find Steve once again in his apartment. It's early morning. Steve, in his robe, makes coffee; he looks very tired. Jetlag and 'other' stuff.

A few days have passed by. The doorbell rings. He crosses the living room to the door, opens it, and Greg enters.

"Yo, dude," Greg says. "How you doing, man? What, you been up all night?"

"I've tried. I mean...long night. So, what's new?"

"No, no, no - this isn't about me, you're the man of the hour! Come on, how'd it go in New York? You nail that job good?"

"Ah...you could say that. I signed the contract, and they're starting things up this week," Steve says, excited, but tired.

"Yee-ha! Oh, we have to celebrate. I'm going to call the whole gang together. We are truly painting this town red," says Greg, very excited.

"Easy, Greg. This is only a first step. Let's not go off half-cocked – I've been doing that most of the night. I mean... this is only the first step, you know?"

"What are you saying?" Greg asks.

Steve waits before responding and then, "Just because I'm getting published, doesn't mean I'm going to be the next Rowling or King. It's a long, hard road ahead."

"Yeah-yeah. Okay, I get the point. Still, you're getting published - that's cause for celebration. Now, come on - tonight, we party. Okay, my man?" Greg asks.

"Yeah – okay," Steve says confirming.

"Now, how about we get to work? We've got some changes to the website to review, before I give them to Larry to input. So, let's-" Greg trails off, motioning to the door.

"Ah...how about later, Greg? I've got a few...positions to work on right now?" Steve asks.

"Ah...Okay, sure, man. Yeah, why not? You deserve a break today - you've earned it. Okay, I'll call you later," says Greg, walking out Steve's apartment door.

After Greg leaves, Steve sits down to work and checks his phone. While reviewing his notes, he discovers the old note titled "Jan Project" and looks off into the distance.

Later that same day Steve goes to the small office, Greg found for the company in a strip mall. A large open space with picture windows looking over the parking lot and a small bathroom and kitchen area in the back.

Steve, Greg, and the leasing agent, the OWNER, enter and start to look around.

"And here," the owner announces, "is the last place I own. It has good square footage, and is centrally located; so you can get to downtown in about two minutes - even just walking!"

"Very nice place. What do you think, Steve?" Greg asks.

"I like that it's got a Sub Shack next door." Steve says, purely thinking about his stomach now.

"Oy! Yeah - great - wonderful. Steve, come on, man - focus."

"Yeah, sorry, dude. It's just that Hillary has kept me... jumping, what with the book - and all," Steve complains.

"Ah, "Project Hillary" - okay, that's a valid excuse. When's the first signing?" Greg asks.

"This weekend at the bookstore right on Colonial Drive," Steve answers.

The owner steps forward, curious, and says "Book signing? Are you an author, sir?"

Greg speaks up first. "Yes, Steve here just wrote a book on making money - how to become a millionaire, legal and illegal ways. The publisher thinks it's a winner, and it kicks off this weekend."

"Really? Well, that's wonderful, congratulations! I'll have to stop by and get a copy." The owner says.

"So, are you interested in the office space?"

Steve nods at Greg, giving the green light and his approval.

Greg changes his tone and says flatly, "Yes, fine. Come on, let's sign the lease."

The Owner opens her briefcase, pulls out a lease and hands it to them.

"Splendid! You boys will not regret this."

"I agree! Well, Steve, looks like we're on our way up."

"Yeah. So...just how big will we get to be?" Steve's mind wanders off into another one of his daydreams.

He can't but imagine the small office growing into a huge, towering office building, scraping the skyline of a major city.

The huge towering office building on the top floor of the office building. A massive desk sits against the far wall, which is all glass and looks out over the city. The room is full of fancy furniture and file cabinets.

Steve, in an Armani suit, sits at his desk. His first secretary sits on the other side of the desk in front of him. His second secretary stands next to Steve. His third secretary puts files in the cabinet while the fourth secretary takes files out of another cabinet.

"All right, send out those letters, file those files, and get me some more coffee," Steve commands.

"Yes, sir!" Shout the secretaries in unison.

The Secretaries get about working. Greg comes in.

"Ah, Steve, I hate to burst your bubble, but-" says Greg.

"Then don't!" Shouts Steve.

"But I have to! The rent, taxes and insurance on this building are killing us. Plus, all the staff - their pay, insurance and benefits are also killing us. We can't afford to maintain this any longer!" Yells Greg.

Suddenly, two U.S. Marshalls enter with guns drawn.

"I'm sorry, gentlemen, but you're under arrest for tax evasion," announces the lead Marshall.

Back in the small Orlando strip mall office, Steve shakes his head and rubs his eyes.

"Huh, maybe we should avoid getting too big." Steve says to himself quietly.

Steve and Greg sign the lease.

Inside Hillary's office, Hillary sits and talks on the phone. On her desk are various promotional artworks for Steve's book and press releases. There's also a copy of the local newspaper, and an article about Steve is on the page.

"Yes, everything came in today; I'll have Steve look them over and then we'll head out," Hillary says.

"Oh, don't you worry, Steve is very excited about the whole process. If this book does half as well as I expect, he's going to be a very wealthy man, and he deserves every bit of it."

Just then, there is a knock at Hillary's office door.

"Ah, I bet that's my boy now. So, got to go," Hillary announces.

Hillary hangs up and rises, quickly smoothing down her hips, and throwing her head back to shake her hair into some sort of place.

"Come in!" She says.

Steve enters and crosses to Hillary, but she doesn't embrace him. She gestures at the items on her desk.

"Hey, Hillary, is everything... going okay?" Steve asks.

"Oh, is this all of the promotional stuff?" Steve asks, looking at Hillary.

"Yes, it is. You ready to head to the bookstore?" Hillary asks.

"Yeah, okay. Wow, so, this is it, isn't it?"

"That it is, Steve. We're in phase two - the publishing and promoting, and that's a huge commitment of time, money, resources and effort! Now, are you prepared for that; are you ready to give 110% to this book project?" Hillary asks.

"I am!" He says finally sounding confident.

"Then, let's go!"

Steve and Hillary head out the door.

A beautiful lake surrounded by grass, a meandering path, and lovely shade trees mark the better neighborhoods of Orlando where Hillary lives.

Steve rides in Hillary's car as she drives along the lake. People walk, jog and ride bikes around the area as Hillary guides her luxury car confidently.

Steve begins to think to himself as they drive along. "So, what's going to happen now? Is this the start of something...

big? For some reason, without...Jan, it just doesn't... feel all that big a deal to me."

Hillary drives up and parks outside a large commercial bookstore. She and Steve get out and head for the store.

Many bookcases full of books line a path to a table with stacks of Steve's book sitting under a huge poster with Steve's smiling face on it.

As they enter, Steve sees the poster and blushes. Greg stands next to the table, a big smile on his face, and a line of people wait on the other side of the table.

Greg announces Steve's arrival, "And here he is, the man of the hour, day, week, month, and whatever! Give it up, people."

"Oh, Greg, please!" Says Steve.

The people applaud. Steve blushes even more, even as Hillary and Greg get him to sit down at the table. Steve starts to sign books for the people waiting to see him.

Steve signs book after book. Hillary and Greg chat with customers and help re-stack the table as Steve drinks some water. Later, Greg rubs Steve's right hand, as Hillary replenishes the table full of Steve's book.

"Oh... Thanks, Man. Boy, talk about writer's cramp!" Steve says to Greg.

"If this is any indication of how well this sucker is going to sell, we won't need to rent an office, we can build our own!" Greg says, thrilled at the turnout.

"One thing at a time, Greg. Let's see how this goes, and how...other things develop."

"Others?" Greg asks. "What, you got an idea for another

book, or another website? Or, something else?"

"Neither, I'm...wondering about Hillary, AND Jan."

"Jan? She blew you off weeks ago," Greg asks, confused.

"I know, but...I...can't stop thinking about her," Steve says reminiscing.

"Hey, dude. What you do in your love life is your business, and none of mine. I just don't think she's worth the effort. I mean, what about Hillary?" Greg asks.

"Oh...We've had some laughs, but I'm just not that serious about her. Or, at all, really. She knows it, too. But...how do I...break it off? I mean, she's my publisher! Won't that be kind of awkward?" Steve is concerned, and looking for Greg to give him some advice.

"Uh, yeah. It could be. Steve, this could be bad for business. You need to think about your feelings for Jan, or having fun with Hillary and being rich at the same time. How lucky could any guy be?

Steve starts to daydream again. Steve imagines being back in Hillary's office.

Steve stands in the corner, cowering behind a chair. Hillary stands on her desk, hurling books at him and announces, "How could you? Tossing me aside for some cheap little tart!"

"Now, Hill', we were just having a little fling." He says.

"Don't call me that," she yells. "You're not ever allowed to call me that ever again! I made you, my boy, and I can break you. I can take you out of this world!"

Steve snaps back to reality.

Just then, a young man in his mid-twenties comes up to

the table. Steve looks up at him, and does a double take - the man looks like he could be a model.

Steve says out loud, "Ah... you never know, Greg. Maybe an answer will just fall in her lap, and present an exit for me."

"Yes. We'll see…," Greg says calmly.

"Hey there, fella. How you doing?"

"Ah…fine…Ah…Mr. Lowe. Could you autograph this for me, please?" The young man asks.

Steve shakes his head no, then laughs and nods. "Just kidding, kid. "Sure, no problem."

"You new to the area?" asks Greg.

"As a matter of fact, I am. How did you know?" the young man says.

"You've got a touch of sunburn - sign of a recent arrival," Greg says pointing at his own face.

"And you're from New York, aren't you?" Steve asks.

"Very good! What tipped you off, the accent?" the young man, asks.

"Yeah," Steve says nodding his head.

Hillary has made her way over to the table.

"Steve, come along now, you can't hold up the line."

"Oh, yes, sorry; we were just chatting with…." Steve says looking up again.

Steve motions to the young man. Hillary looks the young man up and down.

"He's new to the area," Greg says softly, and catching on to Steve's thinking.

"Just moved here from New York." Adds Steve.

Hillary begins to smile wider. "Really? That's where I'm originally from."

Steve plays along with her coy attitude and says, "You don't say? What a surprise! Is it a small world, or what?"

Hillary bends over to grab another stack of books. The young man looks her up and down, and moves to help her.

The young man steps a little closer to Hillary. "Here, let me help you with those." He says and puts the books on the table and moves off to the side to chat with Hillary. Steve continues to sign books for other people.

"Well, Steve," Greg says. "Looks like you may have "dodged the bullet" with Hillary."

Steve leans over and says, "Could be. And, believe me - I'm relieved. I just have to wonder about…"

"Jan?" Greg asks. "As I said, your business, and I'll say no more."

A woman steps up to get her book signed. Steve picks up his pen. Steve finishes signing the book. Greg opens his mouth. A new line of people starts to form.

"Greg, say no more," Steve says sarcastically.

"Yeah, you're right," Greg says chuckling.

Steve finishes signing the books. A new line of people starts to form.

"You would have sworn, I'd written "Groundhog Day" or story called "A Day in Hell for a Writer's Hand."

Greg cannot help but laugh.

Back at Jan's art gallery, it is late in the day. Linda is going over the inventory reports as Jan enters.

"Hey, Boss Lady! Long time no see! How was the trip?

When did you get back in town?"

"Today. This morning. I went home, cleaned up, and decided to head in to check up on things. Did my mother call? She's supposed to arrive today or tomorrow from Rio."

Linda picks up a pile of notes.

"Let me look," Linda says.

"Ah, yeah, she did. She won't be here until tomorrow. Steve called a few times, but never left a message. For that matter, he barely gave me a chance to tell him anything! God, the man is almost like a hyperactive puppy."

"That's all I need. Steve and my mother in the same day."

Jan takes the messages.

"I will deal with my mother tomorrow, then. As for Steve, it doesn't matter. It's all over," Jan says, trying not to become emotional.

"You never know. He seems decent enough, just preoccupied," Linda says reassuringly.

"That's putting it mildly! I've never seen a guy so "book smart" who was so "street dumb". It's no wonder Greg helps him out," Jan says

"I know you like him. It's not like me and Larry."

"Huh? Linda, you're off your nut, if you think that. You're having fun with Larry, just like I had my fun with Steve. Part of me was hoping it would go somewhere, but I just don't know now. He doesn't seem to have time for me, so I'm not going to make time for him either. Fair is fair. Can't just sideline people like that, then pick them up when you want to, or when you remember that you forgot they existed and that you left them on the back burner, while you were having fun with someone else. Someone not me."

"Wow. Oprah and Doctor Phil's baby. That was some deep shit."

"Oh, shut up," Jan says, winking at Linda. Jan heads for her office.

Steve continues his promotional book tour by visiting a local radio show. The studio is a nice little room with several couches, a table and chairs, and two doors – on opposite walls from each other. In the studio, Steve waits to go on the air while Larry sits on the couch in the lounge. Linda on his lap. They kiss. Greg walks in.

"Ah-hem!" Greg sounds out loudly.

They stop. Larry leans back from Linda's lips. "Hi there, Greg. We didn't hear you come in," he says, but unembarrassed.

"So I noticed. Been counting each other's teeth with your tongues again, I see," a smirking Greg says.

Linda turns her head towards Greg and says, "That's our business, Greg. He's my man, after no?! Oh, here's your gum back, babe."

Linda opens her mouth, takes gum out and hands it to Larry. He takes it and puts it in his mouth.

"Thanks." Larry says, chewing. Larry gets to his feet. "So, where's Steve; he here yet? He goes on in ten."

"Yeah, he's just going over some notes for the interview," Greg says looking around the room.

Steve enters from a side studio door, and grabs a bottle of water.

Greg smiles and announces, "And, once again, the man

of the hour! Give it up, peeps."

Steve rolls his eyes.

"Oh, Greg, give it a rest - huh?" Steve says. "Now, come on. I want to do this right - and not make an ass of myself live on air."

"Where's Hillary?" Linda asks out of curiosity. "I thought she'd be on hand to...make sure you didn't do just that."

"Ah...she's...busy," Steve says, trying to evade the question.

"Got a new...friend to fill up her...Time?" Greg answers, suggestively.

The on-air voice of Orlando, Dave is in his mid-40's. He is handsome. He comes in from the other door. Dave is the on-air voice of Orlando – 'Big Dave' they call him.

Time is running out before the show is about to start.

"Ah, Larry, good to see you again. These your friends?" Dave says quickly.

Startled, Larry jumps to attention He nods at Steve and Greg. "Yup. This is Greg, and this is Steve. Guys, this is my good bud' Dave. We went to college together."

"Good to meet you," Dave says, his radio voice drifting across the room.

"A pleasure. Larry says good things about you," Steve says seriously.

"Lies, all lies," Dave says laughing. "Anyway, I picked up a copy of your book today - was just about the last copy the store had. I'd say, you've got yourself a real winner here. So, come on in to the studio, and we'll get you ready."

"Sure, thanks," Steve says.

"Go get 'em, tiger! You're our new celebrity," Larry says enthusiastically.

Steve has a good short laugh.

"Please, me?" Steve asks.

"Well...local celebrity!" Greg says.

Greg snatches up a copy of a newspaper with an article about Steve. "I mean, look, you made the paper, man - and not for getting arrested. That makes you a celeb'...for a good reason. If it works for Paris, it can work for you."

"Yeah, well...we'll see," Steve says, looking down.

Steve and Dave exit the room, and head into the main studio. Greg makes himself comfortable on the couch. Linda looks confused.

"So... What's up with, Steve?" asks Linda. "He looks... kind of down. I thought Madam Publisher was keeping him happy? What...she toss him aside?"

"Far from it," Greg says. "He lined her up with a new 'boy toy'."

"Then... why so down?" Linda asks, sincerely.

"Oh... the big dope. I think he's still pining for..." Greg explains.

"Jan!" Linda blurts out.

"I think so," Greg says, nodding

"Huh. Ah...Would you excuse me, babe? Got a...call to make," Linda says.

"Sure, babe. Make it quick though. They're about to start the show."

The lobby is a large open room with many posters of

various radio shows on the walls. Double doors lead outside are opposite the door to the green room.

Linda comes out of the green room and whips out her cell phone in the lobby. She dials.

The studio is located in a typical radio broadcasting station. A glass wall separates the engineer from a room with a round table, radio microphones, and a couple chairs.

Dave and Steve come into the main room, sit down, and put on a pair of headphones.

Dave clears his throat and says, "Okay, we'll be on the air in just a few minutes."

"Dave, we're good to go." The engineer announces from the other side of the glass. "The 'Happy Hour Show' is just wrapping up right now."

Looking at the clock. Dave adjusts his headset, "Yeah, right on time too! Okay, Steve, we'll cut to commercial, then out intro music, and then…we're on the air. LIVE, BABY!!!"

"Oh - really?" Asks Steve, swallowing his heart. "Great."

In the lobby, Linda has called Jan who is now holding her office phone closely to her ear.

"Okay, I'll give it a listen," Jan says reluctantly.

Jan hangs up the phone and switches on the radio. She tunes it to the right station just in time to hear the show – "Dave's Daily Doings" – come on the air.

Dave assumes his on-air voice and says, "Good afternoon, everyone, and welcome to the show. This is your main man Big Dave, and I'm here with Steve Lowe, author of: "How to Become a Millionaire…Legally."

"Ah…Hi." Steve says.

"So, Steve, word on the street is your book is flying off the shelves like a "Harry Potter" novel on opening day. Is that true," Big Dave says with enthusiasm.

"Ah... Yes." Steve says slowly.

"Oh, that big goof!" Jan exclaims listening from her office.

Dave tries a new question, hoping to change the atmosphere, and pump up the show's mood. He asks, "So, tell us, Steve, what first led you to write this book?"

"Well, I met this lady…," Steve starts, trailing off.

"Oh, what, she was your muse?" Dave says, trying to get Steve into interview mode.

"Yeah, she was something special; although…I…didn't know it at the time."

"Yeah - right, little-miss-publisher got his blood pressure - and other things – up," Jan almost yells. Fuming now and staring at the radio.

Dave leans into the microphone. "So, how did she inspire you? Did she give you the seed for the idea for the book?"

Steve starts and trails off again.

"No, actually, she was - back then - just a…business partner. But… we… shared something special… I just…."

Dave leans in closer to the microphone, his voice low. "But you didn't know it at the time?"

Steve's voice starts, then trails off, again. "No, I didn't. You ever have a situation where…you had something really wonderful, and you…didn't know it until…"

"Until it was gone," Dave says finishing Steve's thought.

"Yeah - exactly." Steve says, coming to terms with his

feelings for the first time.

Jan drops her head. Leaving the radio on, she gets up, and heads towards her office door.

Dave pulls back from the microphone, assuming his usual radio voice. "Dude, just about every guy has been in that situation. So, how did she help with you doing this book?"

"You'll just have to read the book's dedication," Steve says, looking into the empty space on the wall behind Dave.

Dave opens the front cover of the book and begins to read. "'To a special lady, the one who made me feel truly loved - Jan.' Wow, guess she was quite a lady."

Speaking to the wall behind Dave again, Steve answers.

"Yeah, still is. I just wish I could make her understand that."

Jan slowly steps back into her office doorway, a look of total surprise envelops her face. She makes her way out of the art gallery; bolting the door behind her, she makes her way toward her car.

Tears are running down Jan's face, and ruining her mascara. "Steve! I thought you…I thought you only saw me as a…as a cash cow," she whispers to herself, swallowing back some tears, and snot.

Dave nods to his engineer through the glass, announcing to the viewers, "And we'll be right back, after this word from our sponsors."

A commercial starts to play. Dave takes a sip from his water bottle, while Steve just about chugs his cup.

"Easy, Steve, go easy on the water. You don't want to have to take a piss too soon," Dave cautions. Your interview is just getting good, Dave thinks to himself, thumbing through Steve's book.

"Okay. Yeah. Right. You have a point, there. I didn't even think of that," Steve says, swallowing the last bit of water in this mouth.

"Hey, you work in this industry long enough, you learn things. You're doing fine, just try to relax, and give me more than one-word answers, okay?" Dave says, sitting upright, getting ready to go back on the air.

"Ah, yes. Okay. I mean, I'll try to be as articulate as possible."

"That's fine, but you also don't have to talk over the audience either, okay?"

Steve nods.

Just then the engineer waves to Dave and Steve and says, "And we're back in three - two - one, you're on!"

Dave takes a deep breath, his radio voice returning, and taking over. "And we're back with Steve Lowe, local author, local businessman, and local boy making good. Let's go to the phone lines and see what people want to say."

Dave pushes one of the flashing buttons on his console. "Hello, you're on the air with Big Dave! What have ya got to say?"

"Hey, Steve, can I call you Steve?" The caller asks.

"Sure, no problem," Steve shrugs to Dave and waits.

"I'm curious, man, you got this whole section in your book about illegal ways to make money, but you don't give the details. How come?" The caller asks with a suspicious voice.

Steve leans into the microphone. "Well, because I don't

think you should be making your money that way. Ah...as my friend Greg says, it's like in that old show 'MacGyver' - they never showed all of the details of how he did things. They didn't want kids to try and do them."

The caller's voice turns angry and he says, "Oh, so, we're the 'kids', huh? And you're going to decide what we should and should not do! Man, that's un-American."

Stunned, Steve asks, "Are you serious? It's un-American to keep someone from breaking the law? Oh please!"

Dave senses a problem with the caller and jumps into the conversation. "Yeah, I'm with you, Steve. Dude, you need to get your head on straight. Let's take another caller." Dave presses a few buttons on his console again and says, "Yo, you're on the air with Dave! What you got to say?"

Jan's voice comes on the line. "Steve, it's me."

Shocked, Steve says, "Ah...Jan? Is it...really you? I thought you were out of town, or going back to New York with your mother."

"I was, but her flight got delayed, and then Linda called and said I should listen to the show."

"I know we only had a... I mean, we didn't exactly talk about everything..." Steve says trying to explain himself. "Why'd you disappear so quickly?"

Jan waits for a moment and then, "I was hurt that it seemed the only reason you were dating me was to get to my money. And, then I saw that 'Jan Project' on your iPhone! What was I supposed to think about that, huh?"

"Oh - ah - you... saw that, huh?"

"Yes, I did!" Jan shouts. Dave winces and grabs his headphones – a little too loud in his ears; he motions to the engineer to adjust the volume on his headset.

Steve closes his eyes and speaks sincerely. "I'm sorry, Jan. I didn't mean anything by it. That's just how Greg talks about people, talks about projects and work, and my relationships."

"So what about my Mother, and her money?" Jan asks calmly tapping her foot, holding the phone tightly against her cheek.

"Well, we did want it, but then," Steve says searching for the right words, "other things started popping for us, and this book came along. So, I found I... I tried to call...I tried to call...I..."

"Missed me? Yeah, so did I. But you never left a message, Steve." Jan says coldly.

"I didn't know what to say. It doesn't matter now, Jan. Is there any chance we could talk?" Steve asks.

Jan comes into the booth and stands behind the Engineer. She has been in the radio station the whole time. She hangs up her phone and speaks to the Engineer. He smiles and nods. Steve hangs his head.

Dave sees her, but plays along with Jan and says to Steve, "Sorry, man, she hung up."

"So, I guess..." Steve begins.

Meanwhile, in the control room the Engineer flips a switch and turns on the overhead microphones to listen to the conversation and broadcasts it across the airwaves.

"So, tell me more about your book." Jan asks.

Steve practically falls out of the chair as he looks up to see Jan standing there behind the glass, next to the Engineer.

"I can't believe I was so stupid." Steve says. "I got so

caught up in the work that I lost sight of what was important, what was right in front of me. And now, with my book coming out, I'm starting to get some perspective on what's important in life."

Steve gets up and starts to cross to the glass wall. He gets to the limit of the cord for his headset, and he's pulled over backwards. Jan lets out a squeal of concern, bolting for the door separating the Engineer from the others.

Dave helps Steve up as Jan comes in. She takes his hands in hers. Jan puts her hand over Steve's mouth.

"No, Honey, don't say any more. We both screwed up. I say we start over. What do you say?"

"I say this." Steve kisses her passionately. Greg, Linda, and Larry arrive in the booth. They stand with the Engineer and smile.

"So, looks like you two are happy together!" Greg says proudly.

Jan and Steve stop kissing.

"How about a little privacy?" Steve says, smiling at Jan.

"I figured what out from what you I heard you say, but buddy," Greg says motioning to the ceiling and the booth.

"Huh?" Steve grunts looking up at the speakers and mics in the ceiling, and then over at the booth.

"You're on the air, Steve. Remember?" Dave announces to the room.

"Oh, yeah. Right." Steve looks confused.

Jan understands and says, "Come on, Steve. Guys? Let's pick this up after the show, right where we left off."

"Okay, we'll all go out together to some place nice," Steve says, laughing and holding Jan close to his side.

Greg is relieved and ready to party. "Now you're talking, man." He says, turning toward the door, but Dave has airtime to fill and looks worried.

"Hey, what about my show?" Dave asks.

"Oh, yeah…" Steve says and looks around the room.

Steve and Jan kiss again, the part. She goes out to stand with the others in the Engineer's room. Steve sits down in his chair, and puts his headset back on.

"Sorry about that, Dave. Where were we?" Steve asks, sounding like an old media pro.

"Hey, don't apologize, dude, you've got the call in lines lit up like a Christmas tree!" Big Dave is thrilled and looks across his lit up console. Dave pushes a flashing button, quickly choosing a caller. "And you're on the air with Dave and Steve."

Soon after the radio show, the sale of Steve's book skyrocket and his wealth grows, but he is not ready to give up his small apartment just yet. In fact, the little apartment has become a refuge for Steve and Jan as we find Jan posing for Steve, nude. She sits on the bed with a sheet wrapped around her lower body with her back to Steve, who stands at his easel, paints her portrait with great feverish strokes.

Jan is smiling to herself when she says, "So, you finally have enough leisure time to learn how to paint."

"Yeah, it's yet another outlet for my creativity. Ah, I don't know how good it's going to end up looking, but it sure is fun." Steve looks closely at her. "I can't get over the odd events that helped to bring us back together; your mother's flight delayed, Linda being at the radio station and calling you."

"It's like Linda was telling me," Jan begins, "sometimes the strangest events come together."

"To produce the wildest outcomes. That's funny. Larry told me the same thing."

"That's where she said she heard it. One night while he was...Ah, never mind. When does the book tour start?" Jan asks, softly.

"Hillary says about two to three weeks," Steve says, continuing to paint. "She says that book sales are going great, and we're set to hit New York, Chicago, and LA - just to start. You okay with going with me?"

"Are you kidding? Oh, I can't wait until we hit New York. You are getting the grand tour, and introductions to all the right people," Jan says with confidence.

"Well-well, sounds totally awesome; I can't wait!"

"I don't mind posing nude, but are you going to be okay with other people seeing me like this?" Jan asks.

"Oh, I wouldn't worry about that. Come have a look."

Steve stops painting. Jan pulls a robe on and walks over to the easel.

"What the? If you're painting me that way, why did you want me to pose nude?" Jan says a little frustrated.

Steve grins.

They both look at the stick woman on the paper.

"I just like to look at you," he says, laughing.

"Oh you!" she says, wrapping her body around him. Giggling, she kisses him.

THE END

* * *

www.ingramcontent.com/pod-product-compliance
Lightning Source LLC
Chambersburg PA
CBHW071233170626
46809CB00008BA/3031